FAMILY TREE

Contents

edited by Miriam Hodgson

FAMILY TREE
Stories about the family

Mammoth

Contents

First published in Great Britain 1999
by Mammoth, an imprint of Egmont Children's Books Limited
239 Kensington High Street, London W8 6SA

My Father is a Polar Bear copyright © 1999 Michael Morpurgo
Pressed Flowers copyright © 1999 Tim Bowler
Fabric Crafts copyright © 1999 Anne Fine
Just Like Your Father copyright © 1999 Jacqueline Wilson
A Proper Boy copyright © 1999 Vivien Alcock
The Old Team copyright © 1999 Helen Dunmore
Someone Else's Father copyright © 1999 Julie Myerson
We've Got You For Life copyright © 1999 Anthony Masters
On the Bench copyright © 1999 Stephen Potts
Coming Home copyright © 1999 Melvin Burgess
This volume copyright © 1999 Egmont Children's Books Ltd

The moral rights of the authors have been asserted.

ISBN 0 7497 3684 4

10 9 8 7 6 5 4 3 2 1

A CIP catalogue record for this title
is available from the British Library

Typeset by Avon Dataset Ltd, Bidford on Avon, B50 4JH
Printed in Great Britain by Cox & Wyman Ltd, Reading, Berkshire

My Father is a Polar Bear

Michael Morpurgo

Tracking down a polar bear shouldn't be that difficult. You just follow the pawprints – easy enough for any competent Innuit. My father is a polar bear. Now if you had a father who was a polar bear, you'd be curious, wouldn't you? You'd go looking for him. That's what I did, I went looking for him, and I'm telling you he wasn't at all easy to find.

In a way I was lucky, because I always had two fathers. I had a father who *was* there – I called him Douglas; and one who wasn't there, the one I'd never even met – the polar bear one. Yet in a way he *was* there. All the time I was growing up he was there inside my head. But he wasn't only in my head, he was at the bottom of our Start-Rite shoebox, our secret treasure box, with the rubber bands round it, which I kept hidden at the bottom of our cupboard in our bedroom. So how, you might ask, does a polar bear fit into a shoebox? I'll tell you.

My big brother Terry first showed me the magazine under the bedclothes, by torchlight, in 1948 when I was five years old. The magazine was called 'Theatre World'. I couldn't read it at the time, but he could. (He was two years older than me, and already mad about acting and the theatre – he still is.) He had saved up all his pocket money to buy it. I thought he was crazy. 'A shilling! You can get about a hundred lemon sherbets for that down at the shop,' I told him. Terry just ignored me and turned to page twenty-seven. He read it out: *'The Snow Queen*, a dramat . . . something or other . . . of Hans Christian Andersen's famous story, by the Young Vic Company.' And there was a large black and white photograph right across the page – a photograph of two very fierce looking polar bears baring their teeth and about to eat two children, a boy and a girl, who looked very frightened. 'Look at the polar bears,' said Terry. 'You see that one on the left, the fatter one? That's our dad, our real dad. It says his name and everything – Peter Van Diemen. But you're not to tell. Not Douglas, not even Mum, promise?'

'My dad's a polar bear?' I said. As you can imagine, I was a little confused.

'Promise you won't tell,' he went on, 'or I'll give you a Chinese burn.' Of course I wasn't going to tell, Chinese burn or no Chinese burn. I was hardly going to go into school the next day and tell everyone that I had a polar bear for a father, was I? And I certainly couldn't tell my mother, because I knew she didn't like it if I asked about my real father. She always insisted that Douglas was the only father I had. I knew he wasn't, not really. So did she, so did Terry, so did Douglas. But for some reason that was always a complete mystery to me, everyone in the house pretended that he was.

Some background might be useful here. I was born, I later found out, when my father was a soldier in Baghdad during the Second World War. (You didn't know there were polar bears in Baghdad, did you?) Sometime after that my mother met and fell in love with a dashing young officer in the Royal Marines called Douglas Macleish. All this time, evacuated to the Lake District away from the bombs, blissfully unaware of the war and Douglas, I was learning to walk and talk and do my business in the right place at the right time. So my father came home from the war to discover that his place in my mother's heart had been taken. He did all he could to win her back. He took her away on a week's cycling holiday in Suffolk to see if he could rekindle the light of their love. But it was hopeless. By the end of the week they had come to an amicable arrangement. My father would simply disappear, because he didn't want to 'get in the way'. They would get divorced quickly and quietly, so that Terry and I could be brought up as a new family with Douglas as our father. Douglas would adopt us, and give us Macleish as our surname. All my father insisted upon was that Terry and I should keep Van Diemen as our middle name. That's what happened. They divorced, my father disappeared, and at the age of three I became Andrew Van Diemen Macleish. It was a mouthful then and it's a mouthful now.

So Terry and I had no actual memories of our father whatsoever. I do have vague recollections of standing on a railway bridge somewhere near Earl's Court, where we lived, with Douglas' sister – Aunty Betty, as I came to know her – telling us that we had a brand new father who'd be looking after us from now on. I was really not that concerned, not at the time. I was much more interested in the train that was chuffing along under the bridge, wreathing us in a fog of smoke.

My first father, my real father, my missing father, became a taboo person, a big hush-hush taboo person that no one ever mentioned, except for Terry and me. For us he soon became a sort of secret phantom father. We used to whisper about him under the blankets at night. Terry would sometimes go snooping in my mother's desk and he'd find things out about him. 'He's an actor,' Terry told me one night. 'Our dad's an actor, just like Mum is, just like I'm going to be.'

It was only a couple of weeks later that he brought the theatre magazine home and showed it to me, by torchlight, under the blankets. After that we'd take it out again every night and look at our polar bear father. It took some time,

I remember, before the truth of it dawned on me – I don't think Terry can have explained it very well. If he had, I'd have understood it much sooner, I'm sure I would. The truth of course, as I think you might have guessed by now, was that my father was both an actor *and* a polar bear at one and the same time.

Douglas went out to work a lot and when he was home he was a bit silent, so we didn't really get to know him. But we did get to know Aunty Betty. Aunty Betty simply adored us, and she loved giving us treats. She wanted to take us on a special Christmas treat, she said. Would we like to go to the zoo? Would we like to go to the pantomime? There was *Dick Whittington* or *Puss in Boots*. We could choose whatever we liked.

Quick as a flash, Terry said: '*The Snow Queen*. We want to go to *The Snow Queen*.'

So there we were a few days later, Christmas Eve 1948, sitting in the stalls at a matinee performance of the *The Snow Queen* at the Young Vic, waiting, waiting for the moment when the polar bears come on. We didn't have to wait for long. Terry nudged me and pointed, but I knew already which polar bear my father had to be. He was the best one – the snarliest one, the growliest one, the scariest one. Whenever he came on he really looked as if he was going to eat someone, anyone. He looked mean and hungry and savage, just the way a polar bear should look. I have no idea whatsoever what happened in *The Snow Queen*. I simply could not take my eyes off my polar bear father's curling claws, his slavering tongue, his killer eyes. My father was without doubt the finest polar bear actor the world had ever seen. When the great red curtains closed at the end and opened again for the actors to take their bows, I clapped so hard that my hands hurt. Three more curtain calls and the curtains stayed closed. The safety curtain came down and my father was cut off from me, gone, gone for ever. I'd never see him again.

Terry had other ideas. Everyone was getting up, but Terry stayed sitting. He was just staring at the safety curtain as if in some kind of a trance. 'I want to meet the polar bears,' he said quietly.

Aunty Betty laughed. 'They're not bears, dear, they're actors, just actors, people acting. And you can't meet them, it's not allowed.'

'I want to meet the polar bears,' Terry repeated. So did I of course, so I joined in. 'Please, Aunty Betty,' I pleaded. 'Please.'

'Don't be silly. You two, you do get some silly notions sometimes. Have a choc ice cream instead. Get your coats on now.' So we each got a choc ice cream. But that wasn't the end of it.

We were in the foyer, caught in the crush of the crowd, when Aunty Betty suddenly noticed that Terry was missing. She went loopy. Aunty Betty always wore a fox stole, heads still attached, around her shoulders. Those poor old foxes looked every bit as popeyed and frantic as she did, as she plunged through the crowd, dragging me along behind her and calling for Terry. Gradually the theatre emptied. Still no Terry. There was quite a to-do, I can tell you. Policemen were called in off the street. All the programme-sellers joined in the search, everyone did. Of course I'd worked it out. I knew exactly where Terry had gone, and what he was up to. By now Aunty Betty was sitting down in the foyer and sobbing her heart out. Then, cool as a cucumber, Terry appeared from nowhere, just wandered into the foyer. Aunty Betty crushed him to her, in a great hug. Then she went loopy all over again, telling him what a naughty naughty boy he was, going off like that. 'Where were you? Where have you been?' she cried.

'Yes, young man,' said one of the policemen. 'That's something we'd all like to know as well.' I remember to this day exactly what Terry said, the very words. 'Jimmy riddle. I just went for a jimmy riddle.' For a moment he even had me believing him. What an actor! Brilliant.

We were on the bus home, right at the front on the top deck where you can guide the bus round corners all by yourself – all you have to do is steer hard on the white bar in front of you. Aunty Betty was sitting a couple of rows behind us. Terry made quite sure she wasn't looking. Then, very surreptitiously, he took something out from under his coat and showed me. The programme. Signed right across it were these words, which Terry read out to me: 'To Terry and Andrew, with love from your polar bear father, Peter. Keep happy.'

Night after night I asked Terry about him, and night after night under the blankets he'd tell me the story again, about how he'd gone into the dressing room and found our father sitting there in his polar bear costume with his head off (if you know what I mean), all hot and sweaty. Terry said he had a very round, very smiley face, and that he'd laughed just like a bear would laugh, a sort of deep bellow of a laugh – when he'd got over the surprise that is. Terry described him as looking 'like a giant pixie in a bearskin'. For ever afterwards I always held it against Terry that he never took me with him that day down to the dressing room to meet my polar bear father. I was so envious. Terry had a memory of him now, a real memory. And I didn't. All I had were a few words and a signature on a theatre programme from someone I'd never even met, someone who to me was part polar bear, part actor, part pixie – not at all easy to picture in my head as I grew up.

Picture another Christmas Eve fourteen years later. Upstairs, still at the bottom of my cupboard, my polar bear father in the programme in the Start-Rite shoebox; and with him all our other accumulated childhood treasures – a battered champion conker (a 65er!), six silver ball bearings, four greenish silver threepenny bits (Christmas pudding treasure trove), a 'Red Devil' throat pastille tin with three of my milk teeth cushioned in yellowy cotton wool, and my collection of 27 cowrie shells gleaned over many summers from the beach on Samson in the Scilly Isles. Downstairs, the whole family were gathered in the sitting room – my mother, Douglas, Terry and my two sisters (half-sisters really, but of course no one ever called them that), Aunty Betty, now married, with twin daughters, my cousins, who were truly awful. We were decorating the tree, or rather the twins were fighting over every single dingly-dangly glitter ball, every strand of tinsel. I was trying to fix up the Christmas tree lights which of course wouldn't work, whilst Aunty Betty was doing her best to avert a war by bribing the dreadful cousins away from the tree with a Mars Bar each. It took a while, but in the end she got both of them up onto her lap, and soon they were stuffing themselves contentedly with Mars Bars. Blessed peace.

This was the very first Christmas we had had the television. Given half a chance we'd have had it on all the time. But, wisely enough I suppose, Douglas had rationed us to just one programme a day over Christmas. He didn't want the Christmas celebrations interfered with by 'that thing in the corner', as he called it. By common consent, we had chosen the Christmas Eve film on the BBC at five o'clock.

Five o'clock was a very long time coming that day, and when at last Douglas got up and turned on the television, it seemed to take for ever to warm up. Then, there it was on the screen: *Great Expectations* by Charles Dickens. The half-mended lights were at once discarded, the decorating abandoned, as we all settled down to watch in rapt anticipation. Maybe you know the moment. Young Pip is making his way through the graveyard at dusk, mist swirling around him, an owl screeching, gravestones rearing out of the gloom, branches like ghoulish fingers whipping at him as he passes, reaching out to snatch him. He moves through the graveyard timorously, tentatively, like a frightened fawn. Every snap of a twig, every barking fox, every aarking heron sends shivers into our very souls. Suddenly, a face! A hideous face, a monstrous face, looms up from behind a gravestone. Magwitch, the escaped convict, ancient, craggy and crooked, with long white hair and a straggly beard. A wild man with wild eyes, the eyes of a wolf. The cousins screamed in unison, long and loud, which broke the tension for all of us and made us laugh. All except my mother. 'Oh my God,' she breathed, grasping my arm. 'That's your father! It is. It's him. It's Peter.'

All the years of pretence, the whole long conspiracy of silence, were exposed in that one moment. The drama on the television paled into sudden insignificance. The hush in the room was palpable. Douglas coughed. 'I think I'll fetch some more logs,' he said. My two half-sisters went out with him, in solidarity I think. So did Aunty Betty and the twins; and that left my mother, Terry and me alone together. I could not take my eyes off the screen. After a while I whispered to Terry, 'He doesn't look much like a pixie to me.'

'Doesn't look much like a polar bear either,' Terry replied. At Magwitch's every appearance I tried to see through his make-up (I just hoped it *was* make-up!) to discover how my father really looked. It was impossible. My polar bear father, my pixie father, had simply become my convict father.

Until the credits came up at the end my mother never said a word. Then all she said was, 'Well, the potatoes won't peel themselves, and I've got the brussel sprouts to do as well.' Christmas was a very subdued affair that year, I can tell you.

They say you can't put a genie back in the bottle. Not true. No one in the family ever spoke of the incident afterwards – except Terry and me of course. Everyone behaved as if it had never happened. Enough was enough. Terry and I decided it was time to broach the whole forbidden subject with our mother, in private. We waited until the furore of Christmas was over, and caught her alone in the kitchen one evening. We asked her point blank to tell us about him, our 'first' father, our 'missing' father. 'I don't want to talk about him,' she said. She didn't even want to look at us. 'All I know is that he lives somewhere in Canada now. It was another life. I was another person then. It's not important.' We tried to press her, but that was all she would say.

Soon after this I became very busy with my own life, and for some years I thought very little about my convict father, my polar bear father. By the time I was thirty I was married with two sons, and was a teacher trying to become a writer, something I had never dreamt I could be. Terry had become an actor, something he had always been quite sure he would be. He rang me one night very late in a high state of excitement. 'You'll never guess,' he said. 'He's here! Peter! Our dad. He's here, in England. He's playing in *Henry IV, Part II*, in Chichester. I've just read a rave review. He's Falstaff. Why don't we go down there and give him the surprise of his life?'

So we did. The next weekend we went down to Chichester together. I took my family with me. I wanted them to be there for this. He was a wonderful Falstaff; big and boomy, rumbustious and raunchy, yet full of pathos. My two boys (aged ten and eight) kept whispering at me every time he came on. 'Is that him? Is that him?' Afterwards we went round to see him in his dressing room. Terry said I should go in first, and on my own. 'I had my turn a long time ago, if you remember,' he said. 'Best if he sees just one of us to start with, I reckon.'

My heart was in my mouth. I had to take a very deep breath before I knocked on that door. 'Enter.' He still sounded boomy, still Falstaffian. I went in. He was sitting at his dressing table in his vest and braces, boots and britches, and humming to himself as he rubbed off his make-up. We looked at each other in the mirror. He stopped humming, and swivelled round to face me. For some moments I just stood there looking at him. Then I said, 'Were you a polar bear once, a long time ago, in London?'

'Yes.'

'And were you once the convict in *Great Expectations* on the television?'

'Yes.'

'Then I think I'm your son,' I told him.

There was a lot of hugging in his dressing room that night, not enough to make up for all those missing years maybe. But it was a start.

My mother's dead now, bless her heart, but I still have two fathers. I get on well enough with Douglas, I always have done in a detached sort of way. He's done his best by me, I know that, but in all the years I've known him he's never once mentioned my other father. It doesn't matter now. It's history best left crusted over I think.

We see my polar bear father – I still think of him as that – every year or so, whenever he's over from Canada. He's well past eighty now, still acting for six months of every year – a real trouper. My children and my grandchildren always call him 'Grandpa Bear' because of his great bushy beard (the same one he grew for Falstaff!), and because they all know the story of their grandfather, I suppose.

Recently I wrote a story about a polar bear – I can't

imagine why. He's upstairs now, reading it to my smallest granddaughter. I can hear him up there, a-snarling and a-growling just as proper polar bears do. Takes him back, I should think. Takes me back, that's for sure.

Pressed Flowers

Tim Bowler

Being a girl of fourteen isn't much fun sometimes when you want to go out with your friends and instead you've got to look after your three-year-old brother. Not that I dislike Josh. I love him. But he's demanding. He asks questions all the time. Yak, yak, yak. Hannah this, Hannah that. He never asks Mum or Dad. Always me. And because Mum and Dad reckon I handle him well, I get to look after him more than I should.

But a few months ago I was glad I was with him to answer questions because he nearly lost something so precious it would almost have been like losing a life. And in a sense it was about losing a life – though not his.

It was the last week of the summer holidays and Mum came off the phone, her face tense.

'What's wrong?' said Dad.

'That was a Mrs Willet.'

'Who's she?'

Mum hesitated. 'Bill's next-door neighbour.'

'What did she want?'

Mum walked over and put an arm round him.

'I'm sorry, darling. He's dead.'

There was a silence. Then Josh looked up from the floor where he was playing with his model cars.

'So won't he be sending any more Christmas cards?'

Mum looked down at him.

'No, Josh, I'm afraid he won't.'

And in a sense, that was what Uncle Bill had come to mean, certainly as far as Josh was concerned. He had never seen Uncle Bill; and neither had the rest of us since he moved away from our part of Chiswick to Dorset four years ago, breaking off all contact, apart from Christmas cards. It had been a sad thing for me. I used to love Uncle Bill.

You'd never have thought he was Dad's younger brother. They were so different. Dad was tall, dark and neat, a civil servant and a family man. Uncle Bill was a confirmed bachelor, short and chunky with wild wisps of blond hair all over his face; a sculptor with grandiose plans that never came to anything.

He was always in and out of our lives, and not just to borrow money from Dad. He'd come and talk to us about a sculpture he was working on, or ask Dad's advice about some crazy scheme he had for promoting his work, or sit with me in the garden talking about books or films; or sometimes he'd just come over and monkey about like a big kid.

But now he was dead and we were in the car, heading for Dorset.

Josh was with me on the back seat and I was reading him a story. He loves stories; can't get enough of them. He can't read yet but he likes looking at the pictures and, yes, he asks questions all the time. It drives me nuts.

'But why's the wolf hiding behind the hedge?'

'If we read on, Josh, we'll find out.'

'Is it 'cause the pigs are coming home from the market?'

'Well, maybe.'

'Does the wolf want to catch them?'

'Josh, if you'll just let me –'

'But does he?'

'Yes, all right, Josh, he does. He wants to catch them.'

'So why don't they go home another way?'

I rolled my eyes. 'Josh, if we read on, we'll find out.'

Then he wanted to know about Uncle Bill.

'But why did he move away from Chiswick?'

'He just did,' I said.

'It's not fair. You all knew Uncle Bill and I didn't.'

Dad glanced round and smiled at him. 'Don't worry, Josh. He was a bit peculiar.'

'Hannah liked him.'

'We all liked him,' said Dad quickly. 'It's not that. It's just that he sort of changed and moved away to Dorset and didn't want to see us any more.'

Josh looked out of the window. 'What's that sign say?'

'Sherborne. We're nearly there.' Dad looked at Mum. 'Which way?'

Mum checked the map. 'Take the Yeovil road.'

Josh looked at them, his big eyes squinting, then turned back to me. 'You stopped reading,' he said reproachfully.

Bradford Abbas was a sleepy little village. We pulled up outside the shop and I went in with Dad to ask for The Haven. Five minutes later we were outside a small cottage at the edge of the village. A surly-looking woman was dead-heading roses next door.

We climbed out of the car.

'Mrs Willet?' said Dad.

'What of it?'

'I'm Tony James. Bill's brother.'

'Oh.'

'This is my wife, Linda, this is Hannah and this is Josh.'

Mrs Willet nodded vaguely in our direction and continued dead-heading the roses. Dad cleared his throat.

'I believe you have the key.'

Mrs Willet turned and disappeared into her cottage. Josh took my hand.

'Hannah, why's that woman being horrible?'

'She's not being horrible. She's just not very happy.'

'Why not?'

'She just isn't.'

'Why's she gone away?'

'To get the key to Uncle Bill's house.'

'I don't like her.'

I leaned down and whispered, 'Neither do I, Josh, but keep your voice down.'

'What for?'

'She's coming back.'

Mrs Willet came over to the garden wall and handed Dad a slip of paper. 'That's the address of the undertaker.'

'Thank you. Er . . . who found the body?'

'I did. He was slumped over the kitchen table with his face in a plate of bacon and eggs.'

Josh gave a giggle but I squeezed his hand and he was silent.

'How long had he been like that?' said Dad.

'About a month, the man reckoned.'

'A month!' Dad stared at her. 'Didn't anyone notice he wasn't around and do something?'

She shrugged. 'Why should they? We never saw much of him anyway. He often holed up for long periods of time. And you people obviously didn't care much about him or you'd have been trying to get in touch with him.'

Dad bridled at this but Mum put a hand on his arm.

'Let's not get into an argument.' She looked at Mrs Willet. 'Did you find out what he died of?'

Mrs Willet snorted. 'Well, if I drank as much as he did, I'd have been pickled meat long ago.'

'But he hardly ever touched a drop!' said Dad.

That was true. Uncle Bill had had his faults, but drinking was never one of them. Mrs Willet looked Dad over with scorn.

'Just shows how much you've kept in touch since he came here.' She handed Dad a key. 'You'd best be prepared for a shock.'

Josh stared up at her. 'Will it be an electric shock?'

'Nothing so pleasant, lad,' she said, and turned back to her roses.

We followed Dad to the front door of Uncle Bill's cottage.

'I can't believe Bill would have turned to drink,' he said under his breath. 'I mean, I know he went a bit off the rails when he moved away, but drink.' He shook his head. 'Doesn't sound right. Well, let's get this so-called shock over with.'

He turned the key and opened the door. My mouth fell open. The entrance was almost impassable. Bags, boxes, broken sculptures, crockery, books, ornaments and all kinds of junk blocked the way. Piles of magazines rose like columns up to the ceiling. There was barely room to squeeze into the hall.

'I don't believe this,' said Dad.

Mum said nothing and I noticed a deep sadness in her face. I was sad, too. Uncle Bill had lived an unconventional life and his house in Chiswick had never been tidy, but this . . . This was not the house of a man in control of his mind.

'Maybe it's only like this in the hall,' said Dad.

He was wrong. Every room was the same picture of utter chaos. You could hardly move, there was so much clutter. The rubbish bins were packed to overflowing. Shelves, cupboards and surfaces were crammed with packets of tea, jars of coffee, cans of beans. Mouldy fruit lay everywhere amid mouse droppings, milk bottles and unwashed cooking utensils. And Mrs Willet had been right: empty whiskey bottles littered the floors.

Dad sighed. 'I suppose there's one thing – this stuff's mostly rubbish. It should be just a question of chucking things away. It's going to take a few days though.' He looked at his watch. 'Let's get some food inside us at the pub and sort out the bed and breakfast. Then we'd better buy a few hundred bin-bags.'

But clearing and chucking turned out to be more difficult than expected. Most of the stuff was indeed rubbish, but every so often we would find something of real value, like a first edition of *The Lord of the Rings*, signed by the author, so we couldn't just throw things out without proper examination. At least we had six days before Dad had to go back to work; but before two of them had passed, we had another problem.

Josh was getting fractious.

It was hardly surprising. He'd been very good to start with and had insisted on carrying little things and putting them in the bin-bags but now he was bored and becoming rebellious. Mum took me aside.

'Hannah, can you stop what you're doing and spend some time with Josh? It's not fair on him, all this, but we've got to get as much done in the time we have. If you can keep him occupied for a bit and let Dad and me work without interruption, I think we'll get on quicker.'

'OK.'

'Thanks, love.'

Mum returned to the mess in the kitchen. I looked at Josh. He had his back to me and was pushing his model car along the wall of the sitting room.

'Josh?'

He looked round.

'Josh, let's play a game.'

'What game?'

'A secret game.' I thought for a moment. 'Let's see who can find something really interesting in one of the upstairs rooms. We'll each go and find something and keep it a secret and then we'll meet outside in the garden and hide behind the hedge out of sight of Mummy and Daddy –'

'And that horrible woman next door?'

'Yes, and that horrible woman next door, and then I'll try and guess what you've got and you can try and guess what I've got.'

Josh considered this. I knew it wasn't a very good game but it was all I could think of on the spur of the moment. To my surprise, he nodded.

'All right. But no looking at what I've got.'

'OK.'

I took his hand and we went upstairs, picking our way over the rubbish on the stairs. Josh found this hard, being so small, so I went first and cleared things to the side. We stopped on the landing and I looked down at him.

'We'll each hunt in a different room. Which room do you want?'

It didn't make much difference; all the rooms were chock-a-block with junk to choose from. He pointed to the main bedroom.

'That one.'

'OK,' I said. 'I'll look in the spare room.'

He disappeared into the main bedroom and I went into the spare room. I could hear him moving about, picking things up and putting them down again. Then there was a long silence.

'Are you OK, Josh?' I called.

'Don't come in. That's cheating.'

'I'm not going to come in. But are you OK?'

'Yes,' came the answer. I recognised the tone. It meant: 'Don't fuss over me.' I put my mind on my own part of the game. There was plenty of junk in here but it was mostly second-hand books.

I pulled one down and glanced at the title. *The Story of Lancelot and Guinevere*. It was tatty and the binding was coming apart. Josh called through to me.

'I've got my secret thing. Have you got yours?'

I glanced down at the book. I needed a bit more time to find something better but I could tell Josh was anxious to get on with the game. I hid the book behind my back and went out onto the landing. Josh was there, his hands also behind his back.

'No looking,' he said.

'I won't. Listen, I'll close my eyes and wait here and you can go out into the garden and wait by the hedge. Then I'll come out and join you.'

'Count to a hundred.'

'All right.' I closed my eyes.

'You're not counting,' he said.

'I am. I'm doing it in my head.'

'Do it properly or I'm not playing.'

'One . . . two . . . three . . .'

I heard him make his way down the stairs, then the back door opened and shut. It seemed to take an age to reach a hundred and I admit I speeded up at the end, but I knew Josh was well in place by that time. I hurried downstairs, meeting Mum and Dad in the hall, each carrying a bin-bag.

'What's Josh doing in the garden?' said Dad.

'We're playing a game. It's a secret game so don't ask him anything.'

Mum gave me a kiss. 'Thanks, Hannah. I don't know what we'd do without you.'

I made my way out into the garden, the book still behind my back. The sun was fierce but I noticed Josh had found a place under the shade of the hedge. He was sitting on the grass, holding something out of sight to his left, his eyes tightly closed. I sat down next to him, keeping my book behind me.

'OK, Josh. You can open your eyes.'

He blinked them open and looked at me.

'Let me guess yours first,' he said.

'All right. Do you want a clue?'

'No.' He thought for a moment. 'It's a bottle.'

'No.'

'Box.'

'No.'

'Book.'

I frowned. This game was going to be over in no time at all. I pulled the book out and showed him. He gave a shout of triumph.

'What's it say?' he said, staring at the cover.

'*The Story of Lancelot and Guinevere.*'

'Who's that?'

I tried to remember the film. 'He was a knight and she was a queen and they fell in love. But she was married to someone else –'

'Who?'

'King Arthur.'

'Who's he?'

'He was a great king.'

'Did he live in Chiswick?'

'I don't think so. But he was married to Guinevere so it meant she and Lancelot could never be happy together.'

'I don't want to read it if it's a sad book.'

'OK.'

His eyes sparkled. 'Guess my secret thing.'

I tried to remember the things I'd seen in the main bedroom the last time I went in. It was certainly as cluttered as all the other rooms. There was even junk all over the bed. It was a wonder Uncle Bill managed to sleep at all.

'A sculpture,' I said.

'No.'

'Pen.'

'No.'

'Newspaper? Magazine?'

'That's two things. You can only guess one at a time.'

'All right. Newspaper?'

'No.'

'Magazine?'

'No.'

I threw out as many things as I could think of. None of them was right. Josh was getting impatient.

'Give me a clue,' I said.

He thought for a while, his brow wrinkled in an elaborate frown.

'Something Mummy likes.'

'Cards!' I said. 'It's a pack of cards.'

He shook his head. 'Do you give up?' he said.

'OK.'

'I win!' He beamed at me. 'I win, right?'

'Yes, Josh, you win. What's your secret thing?'

He reached behind him and pulled out an envelope. There was typing on it and I could see Uncle Bill's name and his old Chiswick address. The envelope had been untidily ripped open at the top. Josh tipped it and something fell onto the grass.

It was a small posy of pressed forget-me-nots. And then I understood: Mum often pressed flowers. Josh's clue had been a good one.

'Where did you find it?' I said.

'Underneath Uncle Bill's pillow.'

No wonder I hadn't seen it in the room. None of us would have seen it. Josh looked up at me. 'There's a letter in it. What's it say?'

'We mustn't read it. It's private.'

'But Uncle Bill's dead.'

I stared at the envelope. It was none of our business, I knew that, but it was just possible there was something important in it, maybe someone Uncle Bill knew who would need to be informed of his death; maybe even someone who had a right to some of his effects. There was no harm in skimming the contents of the letter just to see. I could always stop reading if it was something personal.

'Let me see,' I said.

He handed me the envelope. I pulled out the letter and unfolded it. It was a single sheet, also typed, with no date and no sender's address.

'What's it say?' said Josh again.

I glanced at him.

'Let me just look through it, then I'll tell you.'

I started to read, aware of his eyes upon me and trying to force myself just to skim over it. But in the end I read every word.

'Hannah!' Josh punched me on the arm. 'What's it say?'

I put the letter down and my eye fell on the pressed flowers on the grass. I picked them up.

'It's a very sad letter. Josh . . . you know we said this is a secret game?'

'Yes.'

'Well, can we keep the letter a secret, too? And the flowers?'

'Yes, but what's it say?'

'It's . . .' I looked down. 'It's a bit like Lancelot and Guinevere. Uncle Bill was in love with someone but she was married to somebody else.'

'Who?'

'The letter doesn't say. It's from the woman he was in love with.'

'Who's that?'

'It doesn't say that either. It's not signed.'

'But what does she say?'

'She says she still cares for him but she can't see him any more because she loves her husband too much.'

'Why's she sent him pressed flowers?'

'To remember her by, I suppose.'

Josh was silent for a long time, the sun playing over his face. Then he spoke again. 'Is that why Uncle Bill drank?'

'Maybe. We'll never know. Come on, let's find some more secret things.'

'I don't want to play any more.'

'OK.' I looked down at the letter and tried to think how to phrase what I had to say next. But Josh solved the problem for me.

'I don't want to keep the letter if it's sad,' he said.

'All right, I'll look after it. But it's got to be a secret, right? Not a word to a soul, not even Mummy and Daddy.'

'Where's my car?' he said, looking around him. 'I brought it out with me.'

I smiled. He'd forgotten about the letter already.

'You left it in the sitting room on top of the television.'

He jumped up and ran back to the house. I waited until he had disappeared inside, then put the flowers in my pocket and read the letter again.

Dear Bill,

It's no good us pretending. You know I'll never leave him. I love him too much. And deep down we both know that what happened was wrong. Somehow you must let me go. But Bill, if you care for me, do one last thing for me – one big thing. And don't hate me for asking it.

I want you to let the child go, too. I've never told T what the doctor said to me after his operation, so he thinks he's still fertile and that the baby I'm carrying is his. He's so yearned for this second child. Don't shatter that for him.

Your future is not with me. You know that. It's with your work and your dreams. And mine is here, with T and H, and our new baby.

God bless you.

L.

I put the letter down, my mind on Josh, and my eyes swimming with tears. Inside the house I could hear Josh and Dad laughing. They were wrestling probably, a favourite game. I waited for several minutes, then wiped my eyes, put the letter back in the envelope, and walked towards the house. Mum came out, carrying a bin-bag to stack with the others in front of the garage.

'Hold on, Mum.' I scrumpled the envelope behind my back, then reached into the bag and thrust it far down inside. Mum didn't see. She was looking at the book in my other hand. She smiled.

'*Lancelot and Guinevere*. That's a sad story.'

'I know.'

She put her arm round me.

'Are you all right, darling?'

'Fine.'

'Anything else to throw away?'

I fingered the flowers in my pocket, then shook my head. 'No, Mum. Nothing else.'

'Thanks for spending time with Josh. He looks as though he'll be OK now.'

I glanced away, my hand still on the flowers, and watched the swallows playing in the late-summer light.

'Yes,' I said. 'He'll be OK.'

Fabric Crafts

Anne Fine

Alastair MacIntyre gripped his son Blair by the throat and shook him till his eyes bulged.

'Look here, laddie,' he hissed. 'I'm warning ye. One more time, say that one more time and whatever it is ye think ye're so good at, *whatever*, I'll have ye prove it!'

'You let go of Blair at once,' said Helen MacIntyre. 'His breakfast's getting cold on the table.'

Giving his son one last fierce shake, Alastair MacIntyre let go. Blair staggered backwards and caught his head against the spice shelf. Two or three little jars toppled over and the last of the turmeric puffed off the shelf and settled gently on his dark hair.

Alastair MacIntyre heard the crack of his son's head against the wood and looked up in anguish.

'Did ye hear that? Did ye hear that, Helen? He banged his head on yon shelf. He couldnae have done that a week back. The laddie's still growing! It'll be new trousers in another month. Och, I cannae bear it, Helen! I cannae bear to watch him sprouting out of a month's wages in clothes before my eyes. I'd raither watch breakfast telly!'

And picking up his plate, he left the room.

'What was all that about?' Blair asked his mother, rubbing his head. 'Why did he go berserk? What happened?'

'You said it again.'

'I didnae!'

'You did.'

'How? When?'

'You came downstairs, walked through the door, came up behind me at the stove, looked over my shoulder at the bacon in the pan, and you said it.'

'I didnae!'

'You did, lamb. You said: "I bet I could fit more slices of bacon into the pan than that". That's what you said. That's when he threw himself across the kitchen to throttle you.'

'I didnae hear myself.'

Helen MacIntyre put her hands on her son's shoulders and raised herself onto her tiptoes. She tried to blow the turmeric off his hair, but she wasn't tall enough.

'No. You don't hear yourself. And you don't think before you speak either. I reckon all your fine brains are draining away into your legs.'

'Blair doesnae have any brains.' Blair's younger sister, Annie, looked up from her crunchy granola. 'If he had any brains, he wouldnae say the things he does.'

'I dinnae say them,' Blair argued, fitting his long legs

awkwardly under the table. 'They just come out. I dinnae even hear them when they're said!'

'There you are,' Annie crowed. 'That's what Mum said. All legs, no brain.'

She pushed her plate away across the table and dumped her school bag in its place. 'Tuesday. Have I got everything I need? Swimsuit, gymshorts, metalwork goggles, flute and embroidery.'

'Wheesht!' Blair warned. 'Keep your voice down.' But it was too late. The cheery litany had brought Alastair MacIntyre back into the doorway like the dark avenging angel of some ancient, long-forgotten educational system.

'Are ye quite sure ye've no forgotten anything?' he asked his daughter with bitter sarcasm. 'Skis? Sunglasses? Archery set? Saddle and bridle, perhaps?'

'Och, no!' said Annie. 'I won't be needing any of them till it's our class's turn to go to Loch Tay.'

Alastair MacIntyre turned to his son.

'What about you, laddie? Are you all packed and ready for a long day in school? Climbing boots? Beekeeping gear? Snorkel and oxygen tank?'

'Tuesday,' mused Blair. 'Only fabric crafts.'

'Fabric crafts?'

'You know,' his wife explained to him. 'Sewing. That useful little skill you never learned.'

'Sewing? A laddie of mine sitting at his desk sewing?'

'No, Dad. We dinnae sit at our desks. We have to share

the silks and cottons. We sit round in a circle, and chat.'

'Sit in a circle and sew and chat?'

Blair backed away.

'Mam, he's turning rare red. I hope he's no' going to try again to strangle me!'

Alastair MacIntyre put his head in his hands.

'I cannae believe it,' he said in broken tones. 'My ain laddie, the son and grandson of miners, sits in a sewing circle and chats.'

'I dinnae just chat. I'm very good. I've started on embroidery now I've finished hemming my apron!'

Alastair MacIntyre groaned.

'His apron!'

'Dinnae take on so,' Helen MacIntyre comforted her husband. 'Everyone's son does it. The times are changing.' She tipped a pile of greasy dishes into the sink and added: 'Thank God.'

'Not *my* son!' Alastair MacIntyre cried. 'Not *my* son! Not embroidery! No! I cannae bear it! I'm a reasonable man. I think I move with the times as fast as the next man. I didnae make a fuss when my ain lassie took up the metalwork. I didnae like it, but I bore with it. But there are limits. A man must have his sticking place, and this is mine. I willnae have my one and only son doing embroidery.'

'Why not?' demanded Blair. 'I'm very good at it. I bet I can embroider much, much better than wee Annie here.'

A terrible silence fell. Then Annie said:

'Ye said it again!'

Blair's eyes widened in horror.

'I didnae!'

'You did. We all heard ye. You said: "I bet I can embroider much, much better than wee Annie here".'

'I didnae!'

'Ye did.'

'Mam?'

Mrs MacIntyre reached up and laid a comforting hand on his shoulder.

'Ye did, lamb. I'm sorry. I heard it, too.'

Suddenly Alastair MacIntyre looked as if an unpleasant thought had just struck him. He quickly recovered himself and began to whistle casually. He reached over to the draining-board and picked up his lunch box. He slid his jacket off the peg behind the door, gave his wife a surreptitious little kiss on the cheek and started sidling towards the back door.

'Dad!'

Alastair MacIntyre pretended not to have heard.

'Hey, *Dad*!'

Even a deaf man would have felt the reverberations. Alastair MacIntyre admitted defeat. He turned back to his daughter.

'Yes, hen?'

'What about what you told him?'

'Who?'

'Blair.'

'What about, hen?'

'About what would happen if he said it again.'

Alastair MacIntyre looked like a hunted animal. He loosened his tie and cleared his throat, and still his voice came out all ragged.

'What did I say?'

'You said: "Say that one more time and whatever it is you think you're so good at, *whatever*, I'll have ye prove it." That's what you said.'

'Och, weel. This doesnae count. The laddie cannae prove he sews better than you.'

'Why not?'

'He just cannae.'

'He can, too. I'm entering my embroidery for the end-of-term competition. He can enter his.'

'No, lassie!'

'Yes, Dad. You said so.'

'I was only joking.'

'Dad! You were not!'

Alastair MacIntyre ran his finger around his collar to loosen it, and looked towards his wife for rescue.

'Helen?'

Annie folded her arms over her school bag and looked towards her mother for justice.

'Mam?'

Mrs MacIntyre turned away and slid her arms, as she'd

done every morning for the last nineteen years, into the greasy washing-up water.

'I think,' she said, 'it would be very good for him.'

Alastair MacIntyre stared in sheer disbelief at his wife's back. Then he slammed out. The heavy shudder of the door against the wooden frame dislodged loose plaster from the ceiling. Most of it fell on Blair, mingling quite nicely with the turmeric.

'Good for me, nothing,' said Blair. 'I'd enjoy it.'

'I didnae mean good for you,' admitted Mrs MacIntyre. 'I meant it would be good for your father.'

It was with the heaviest of hearts that Alastair MacIntyre returned from the pithead that evening to find his son perched on the doorstep, a small round embroidery frame in one hand, a needle in the other, mastering stem stitch.

'Have ye no' got anything better to do?' he asked his son irritably.

Blair turned his work over and bit off a loose end with practised ease.

'Ye know I've only got a week, Dad. I'm going to have to work night and day as it is.'

Alastair MacIntyre took refuge in the kitchen. To try to cheer himself, he said to Helen:

'Wait till his friends drap in to find him ta'en up wi' yon rubbish. They'll take a rise out o' the laddie that will bring him back into his senses.'

'Jimmy and Iain were here already. He sent them along to The Work Box on Pitlochrie Street to buy another skein of Flaming Orange so he could finish off his border of french knots.'

The tea mug shook in Alastair MacIntyre's hand.

'Och, no,' he whispered.

Abandoning his tea, he strode back into the hall, only to find his son and his friends blocking the doorway as they held one skein of coloured embroidery floss after another up to the daylight.

'Ye cannae say that doesnae match. That's perfect, that is.'

'Ye maun be half blind! It's got a heap more red in it than the other.'

'It has not. It's as yellowy as the one he's run out of.'

'It is not.'

'What about that green, then? That's perfect, right?'

'Aye, that's unco' guid, that match.'

'Aye.'

Clutching his head, Alastair MacIntyre retreated.

The next day, Saturday, he felt better. Ensconced in his armchair in front of the rugby international on the television, his son at his side, he felt a happy man again – till he looked round.

Blair sat with his head down, stitching away with a rather fetching combination of Nectarine and Baby Blue.

'Will ye no' watch the match?' Alastair MacIntyre snapped at his son.

'I am watching,' said Blair. 'You should try watching telly and doing satin stitch. It's no' the easiest thing.'

Alastair MacIntyre tried to put it all out of his mind. France vs Scotland was not a match to spoil with parental disquiet. And when, in the last few moments, the beefy fullback from Dunfermline converted the try that saved Scotland's bacon, he bounced in triumph on the springs of his chair and shouted in his joy:

'Son, did ye see that? Did ye see that!'

'Sorry,' said Blair. 'This coral stitch is the very de'il. Ye cannae simply stop and look up halfway through.'

All through the night, Alastair MacIntyre brooded. He brooded through his Sunday breakfast and brooded through his Sunday lunch. He brooded all through an afternoon's gardening and through most of supper. Then, over a second helping of prunes, he finally hatched out a plan.

The next evening, when he drove home from the pithead, instead of putting the car – a K-registration Temptress – away in the garage he parked it in front of the house and went in search of his wayward son. He found him on the upstairs landing, fretting to Annie about whether his cross-stitches were correctly aligned.

'Lay off that, laddie,' Alastair MacIntyre wheedled. 'Come out and help me tune up the car engine.'

Blair appeared not to have heard. He held his work up for his father's inspection.

'What do you reckon?' he said. 'Be honest. Dinnae spare my feelings. Do ye think those stitches in the China Blue are entirely regular? Now look very closely. I want ye to be picky.'

Alastair MacIntyre shuddered. Was this his son? He felt as if an incubus had taken hold of his first born.

'Blair,' he pleaded. 'Come out to the car. I need your help.'

'Take wee Annie,' Blair told him. 'She'll help ye. She got top marks in the car maintenance module. I cannae come.'

'Please, laddie.'

Alastair MacIntyre was almost in tears.

Blair rose. Extended to his full height, he towered over his father.

'Dad,' he said. 'Take wee Annie. I cannae come. I cannae risk getting oil ingrained in my fingers. It'll ruin my work.'

Barely stifling his sob of humiliation and outrage, Alastair MacIntyre took the stairs three at a time on his way down and out to the nearest dark pub.

He came home to find wee Annie leaning over his engine, wiping her filthy hands on an oily rag.

'Ye've no' been looking after it at all well,' she scolded him. 'Your sparking plugs were a disgrace. And how long is it since you changed the oil, I'd like to know.'

Mortified, feeling a man among Martians, Alastair MacIntyre slunk through his own front door and up to his bed.

On the morning of the school prize-giving, Alastair MacIntyre woke feeling sick. He got no sympathy from his wife, who laid his suit out on the double bed.

Alastair MacIntyre put his head in his hands.

'I cannae bear it!' he said. 'I cannae bear it. My ain son, winning first prize for fabric crafts, for his sewing! I tell you, Helen. I cannae bear it!'

He was still muttering 'I cannae bear it' over and over to himself as the assistant head teacher ushered the two of them to their seats in the crowded school hall. The assistant head teacher patted him on the back in an encouraging fashion and told him: 'You maun be a very proud man today, Mr MacIntyre.'

Alastair MacIntyre sank onto his seat, close to tears.

He kept his eyes closed for most of the ceremony, opening them only when Annie was presented with the Junior Metalwork Prize, a new rasp. Here, to prove he was as much a man of the times as the next fellow, he clapped loudly and enthusiastically, then shut his eyes again directly, for fear of seeing his only son presented with a new pack of needles.

When the moment of truth came, he cracked and

peeped. Surreptitiously he peered around at the other parents. Nobody was chortling. Nobody was whispering contemptuously to a neighbour. Nobody was so much as snickering quietly up a sleeve. So when everyone else clapped, he clapped too, so as not to seem churlish.

Somebody leaned forward from the row behind and tapped on his shoulder.

'I wadna say but what ye maun be a proud faither today, Alastair MacIntyre.'

And raw as he was, he could discern no trace of sarcasm in the remark.

As they filed out of the hall, Annie and Blair rejoined them. Alastair MacIntyre congratulated his daughter. He tried to follow up this success by congratulating his son, but the words stuck in his throat. He was rescued by the arrival, in shorts and shirts, of most of the school football team.

'Blair! Are ye no' ready yet? We're waitin' on ye!'

The goalie, a huge burly lad whose father worked at the coal face at Alastair MacIntyre's pit, suddenly reached forward and snatched at Blair's embroidery. Blair's father shuddered. But all the goalie did was start to fold it up neatly.

'A fair piece o' work, that,' he said. 'I saw it on display in yon hall. I dinnae ken how you managed all them fiddly bits.'

'Och, it was nothing,' said Blair. 'I bet if you tried, you

could do one just as guid.'

Alastair MacIntyre stared at his son, then his wife, then his daughter, then his son again.

'No, no,' demurred the goalie. 'I couldnae manage that. I've no' got your colour sense.'

He handed the embroidery to Alastair MacIntyre.

'Will ye keep hold o' that for him,' he said. 'He's got to come and play football now. We cannae wait any longer.' He turned to Annie. 'And you'll have to come too, wee Annie. Neil's awa' sick. You'll have to be the referee.'

Before she ran off, Annie dropped her new rasp into one of her father's pockets. Blair dropped a little packet into the other.

Alastair MacIntyre jumped as if scalded.

'What's in there?' he demanded, afraid to reach in and touch it in case it was a darning mushroom, or a new thimble.

'Iron-on letters,' Blair said. 'I asked for them. They're just the job for football shirts. We learned to iron in home economics. I'm going to fit up the whole football team.'

'What with?'

'KIRKCALDIE KILLERS,' Blair told him proudly. 'In Flaming Orange and Baby Blue.'

Just Like Your Father

Jacqueline Wilson

'You're just like your father!'

I stared at Mum.

She stared at me. She looked taken aback, as if someone else had taken control of her mouth.

'That's a stupid thing to say.'

'I know,' said Mum. 'I didn't mean it. It's just . . . I don't know who you are any more sometimes, Josh.'

'I don't know either,' I said miserably. I plucked at the sleeves of my sweatshirt. They no longer covered my long bony wrists. 'I need a new one, Mum.'

'But I only got you that one at Christmas. And it wasn't half a price, too.'

Mum gently prodded the designer lettering. I didn't have the heart to tell her it wasn't cool any more, that these very initials spelt nerd and naff this month. I concentrated on unarguable fact.

'It's too small.'

Mum tried pulling it down, like I was a toddler who hadn't quite got the knack of dressing himself.

'Leave it out, Mum!' I said, wriggling free.

'It *is* too small,' she said, sighing, folding her arms as she looked at me. Looked *up* at me.

For the past year I'd been able to see the top of her head. It was weird noticing the little pink patch where her hair parted too determinedly, and the dark mouse of her roots. She tried so hard to keep herself looking good. When she went off with her women friends on Friday nights, all dolled up in too-tight clothes, I got a lump in my throat.

It was worse when she came back at eleven, talking brightly, telling me she'd had a really great night out when she looked so tired and her plum lipstick was smudged. Not with kissing. Mum never seemed to meet up with any men. She said she didn't want to, didn't need a man in her life. She used to say, 'You're the only man for me, Josh.' But that was when I was a little kid.

'You're too big,' she said.

'What?'

'It's you, not the sweatshirt,' Mum said, smiling to show it was a joke. 'When are you going to stop growing?'

'*I* don't know,' I said. 'I wish you wouldn't keep going on about it.'

I was getting a complex. I'd always been a bit on the

small side. Mum often called me Little Titch. We were both sure I took after her. I had her dark-mouse hair and her brown eyes and her neat wiry body. She could still run like the wind for a bus even in her high heels, or vacuum the house from top to bottom, dancing along to her daft old eighties albums, not even out of breath. I'd never been much of a dancer (I was strictly a guy who leant against the wall at the school disco) but I could run fast enough to make the first three on sports day and I was in Mr Townsend's first team for football, which came in useful to establish my Lad credibility.

I had to work hard to avoid any Mummy's Boy taunts. When I was young and stupid I'd burble on about Mum and me going swimming on Saturdays, or Mum and me going up to the Trocadero for a treat, or Mum and me sharing a pizza with six extra toppings for our Sunday lunch. The other kids would roll their eyes and go 'Mum-and-me' in silly prissy voices.

I'd learnt to shut up about Mum and me. Not that we did that much together nowadays. Not that I did anything much with anyone. I moseyed around by myself or lay on my bed for hours, staring, wondering if one day I was going to graze the ceiling when I stood up.

I'd grown six inches in the last six months and I didn't show any sign of stopping. I wondered if my body would ever cotton on that it had grown enough. Maybe my arms would carry on until I could reach all the way up the road and round the corner and my legs would stretch until I could see clear over every tower block and have to bat the birds out of my way.

My head and torso couldn't quite catch up and my shoulders were hunched anyway because I'd started to feel permanently defensive. Mr Townsend wanted me to go along to this gym to work out.

'It's time you developed that growing body, lad. You want to look like a gorilla, not a giraffe.'

I wasn't inspired by either animal, and I was wary of Mr Townsend. He'd never done anything dodgy but I knew he wasn't the sort of guy who liked girls. I didn't act like I was either. I blushed like a beetroot and ran backwards whenever any of the girls at school so much as spoke to me, and I never joined in all the jolly tits-and-bums talk with the other boys in my class – but in bed at nights I thought about girls a lot. That was another worrying area of growth.

There was so much physical activity going on in my body I felt that any minute now I'd go 'twang' like elastic. It didn't help that Mum kept hassling me. Like, 'Do you have to lounge there like a great lump? Couldn't you even put the potatoes on for us? I wouldn't *mind* if you were doing your homework or some kind of hobby. Why don't you have hobbies any more? But it really gets on my nerves when you just lie on that sofa waiting for me to come home from work to fetch and run for you.'

She rabbited on like this and I tried to stare straight past her and concentrate on the wallpaper because it seemed the more peaceful option. She got madder and madder, thumping things around in the kitchen and flexing her arms ostentatiously because she's always scared she'll get Repetitive Strain Injury with all the keyboard work at her Building Society. I made the mistake of yawning in the middle of her sentence. I wasn't being deliberately rude, I was *tired*, but I suppose it looked a little insulting. And that was when she came right out and said it.

'You're just like your father!'

The words seemed to have jammed in my brain. I didn't have a clue what my father was like – apart from the fact that he was an all-time Mr Bad Guy. He left when I was three, right after my mum miscarried my brother-who-never-was. I wish he'd been born. I'd give anything to have a brother, even if we fought all the time. At least it would break up this Mum-and-me thing a bit. But we *were* just Mum-and-me, and Dad had done a runner with some eighteen year old at his work and never bothered to get in touch. Well, once or twice at Christmas. He didn't ever remember birthdays, but there was a full Manchester United football strip when I was about eight – though it was a very little kid's size, so I couldn't wear it without looking ridiculous.

Then there was one of those huge floppy polar bears, grubby round the paws like it had been hanging about a fairground for a few months first. A great mangy toy bear for a boy going on ten. Mum hauled it off to the Oxfam shop the first day it opened after Christmas and I didn't try to stop her – but I missed that bear a lot. When Mum was out in the kitchen basting our mini turkey-for-two I lugged the bear off the floor and buried my face in its off-white nylon fur. Not to hug the *bear*. To try to sniff out some strange smell – an unfamiliar aftershave, cigarettes, booze. I had no idea what my dad smelt like. But the bear smelt synthetically of itself, no help at all.

Mum wasn't much help either. She mostly didn't mention Dad – or when I badgered her she'd speak in jerky little sentences, her face screwed up, as if the words were glass splinters on her tongue. He had curly hair. He had a funny laugh. He liked a drink. When I got older, especially after she'd had a drink or two herself, she'd tell me what he was *really* like: the good looks, the flirting, the drinking – the violence too. She never said, but I sometimes wondered if he'd had anything to do with my brother's miscarriage. I knew he'd not been a great dad with me. He hadn't been *any* kind of a dad.

He hadn't sent presents recently. Not even cards. On my last birthday I didn't even wonder whether there'd be anything from Dad. I didn't *want* anything. I'd cut him out of my life for ever.

But now he seemed to be creeping in through *me*. I'd always thought I had straight hair but when I worried that my crew cut emphasized my new pinhead I discovered my hair grew curly when it got the chance. Mum said she didn't know who I was any more – but we both knew. I was turning into a guy just like my dad and I couldn't stand it.

'I'm going out for a bit, Mum,' I said, suddenly desperate to get out of the house.

'Where? What are you on about? Your tea's nearly ready.'

'I know. I'm sorry. I just . . . I've got to go *out*.'

I went before she could stop me, striding off purposefully though I didn't really have a clue where I was going. I felt mean about Mum. She looked like she was crying when I slammed out of the door. Just like my father. Give me another few years and perhaps I'd be living out my night fantasies. Would I then get some girl into trouble and hit her and yell at her little kid and walk out on them for ever and break their hearts?

I felt as bad as if I'd actually done it already. I kept catching glimpses of myself in shop fronts and car windows until there seemed to be hundreds of big boy-men patrolling the pavements with me, all of them huge, all of them hateful.

I wished I could stop growing. I wished I could shrink back into being a really little kid. Maybe if I'd been a really cute cheeky little chap, Dad might have stayed after all. Maybe he'd have taken me to the park to feed the ducks,

51

and kicked a football about with me, and set me on his knee at nights and told me a story – a fairy story about a beast who was tamed by a little boy so he turned into the handsome prince.

I found I was walking right up to the park gates, as if my big feet with their ever-growing toes crammed up tight inside their trainers had a will of their own. So I gave in and walked once round the park, wishing I had some stale bread for the ducks. There was a little gaggle of girls from my school looking around, quacking louder than the ducks, and when they spotted me they started calling out silly stuff.

'Hey, Josh!'

'Golly gosh, Josh!'

'Where you going, Josh?'

'Come and walk with us, Josh.'

'What's the weather like up there, Josh?'

'What's that on your head, Josh?'

Like a fool I felt my hair. They all shrieked.

'It's a *cloud*, Josh!'

I bared my teeth in a foolish Snoopy grin and rushed right past them, hot all over though it was a dank day and getting even chillier now it was nearly dark.

I sloped off to the kids' playground and sat on a swing, scraping the toes of my trainers backwards and forwards. The playground was empty at first, all the mums and kids gone home for tea. Then this guy came trailing along with a big baby in a buggy. At first glance you'd think he'd be more likely taking a Rottweiler for a walk. The guy was big and brawny and it was a safe bet there were tattoos somewhere under his sweatshirt. He was getting on a bit, his hair greying, his face lined. I wasn't sure if he was Dad or Grandad. He was obviously someone really special to the baby. It was grinning gummily up at him. I didn't know if it was a boy or a girl because it was all wrapped up in its jacket and little dungarees. It had a bag of bread in its damp woolly mittens and it kept on going, 'Quack quack.'

'Yes, quack quack. The ducks go quack quack,' said the man patiently, though he'd obviously said it thirty or forty times since leaving the pond.

'Quack quack,' said the baby.

'Yes, quack quack. You're the little duck. Let's take you home and feed you, little duck, it's getting dark and cold.'

'Quack quack!' said the baby, but then it caught sight of the swings and started wailing.

'No, you don't want a swing now, chum, we've got to go home,' said the man. 'Come on, quack quack.'

But the quack game was out of fashion now. The baby's wail said swing swing swing with increasing urgency.

'Okay, okay, one little swing and then we *must* go home,' said the man.

He patiently unbuckled, unstrapped and unhooked and then sat on the swing himself with the squirmy baby on his lap, gently moving to and fro, to and fro.

We were around the same height so our eyes kept meeting. The man grinned a little foolishly.

'Kids,' he said.

I nodded, as if I were knowledgeable in that area. I wanted to talk some more. I wanted to get to know all about this tall tough guy. I wanted to find out if he really was the grandad. Maybe he was a second-time-around dad and putting in more time with this kid. I thought about my own missing dad.

In the end I didn't say anything. We both swung backwards and forwards and the baby squeaked with delight, waving its soggy mittens in the air. It wailed again when the man eventually bundled it back into the buggy, but then he distracted it with some more duck imitations and they quacked-quacked off together into the dark.

I sat on for a bit, thinking. If the two of them hadn't got on it wouldn't have been the baby's fault. And maybe it wouldn't have been all the guy's fault either. But they did get on. They were a great father and son. I'd had a lousy father but it didn't mean I had to be a lousy father later on.

All this thinking was doing my head in. I decided it was time to make for home too. The girls were still messing around by the duckpond.

I decided to get in before they did. I called out, 'Hey there, little munchkins,' and made them giggle some more. I still blushed, but it was so dark they couldn't see.

All the spring flowers scented the night. I bent over

quickly and plucked a handful to give to Mum when I got back. I strode home in my seven league trainers, happy to have my head in the clouds.

A Proper Boy

Vivien Alcock

Harry's father was a strong man, tall and muscular. He did exercises in front of an open window every morning and when he finished, he slapped his flat stomach four times. Hard. In summer, when Harry's own window was open, he could hear the sound very plainly. The last slap was always the loudest. Harry thought it was meant for him.

His father's name was Victor George Wellington. He had always wanted a son. A son to take to football matches, a son to play cricket with on the beach, to take sailing in small boats, and riding on large horses. He wanted a boy like his brother's son, Marcus, tough, rosy-cheeked, afraid of nothing. It was just his bad luck that he had four daughters, one after another. Victoria, Georgina, Julie and Nell. He was fond of them, of course he was. He was not an ogre. He didn't say, 'Oh no! Not another girl,' when he saw them appear. But everyone knew he had wanted a son.

Harry's mother Isobel wasn't bothered. She thought the girls were fine and didn't want to have another child.

'Babies are tiring,' she told her husband. 'You wouldn't know that, Victor. You've always gone out to work. Going out to work is a rest cure compared to looking after babies and toddlers. I know. I've done both in my time. Besides the world is overpopulated. Four children are enough.'

Victor George Wellington didn't shout at her. He didn't insist. He just looked grave and disappointed, and went on looking disappointed, day after day, week after week, until in the end, she sighed and said, 'Oh, all right, Victor. One more child. One last chance for a boy.'

It was Harry's bad luck that he was that boy.

His sisters, Vicky, Georgie, Julie and Nell were tall, healthy girls, with pink cheeks and bright eyes. Vicky was good at all games. Georgie had a silver medal for swimming, and Julie was a gymnast. Nell, the youngest and softest of his sisters, had recently abandoned her dolls for a cricket bat and a toy gun. Even his mother, though only of average height, was sturdy and strong. But Harry?

To be honest, Harry was more like a stalk of grass than a branch of the family tree. He was small for his age, and spindly. His hair, when it grew, was pale yellow and silky. Left to itself, it curled all over his head like a cherub's, but it was not left to itself for long. His father saw to that.

'For heaven's sake, Isobel, take that boy to have his hair cut. He looks just like a girl,' he would say, and if Mum told him that she was too busy, he took the little boy himself and had his hair cut so short that his head looked like a ping pong ball, and all his sisters laughed and called him a skinhead.

Harry cried.

His father did not shout at him. He took him on his lap and said very gravely, 'Boys don't cry, Harry. Remember. You can't learn that soon enough if you want to grow up into a big, strong man like me. Your cousin Marcus never cries. Try and be like him.'

'For heaven's sake, Victor,' Isobel said. 'He's only six, poor kid. I could cry myself. All those lovely curls gone. Where have you been all your life? Open your eyes next time you go out in the streets. Lots of young men have long curly hair. And very nice they look too.'

'Not my son,' Victor George Wellington said. 'I see I'll have to take him in hand.'

Harry ran upstairs to his room and shut the door behind him. He didn't want his father to take him in hand. It was not that he was frightened of his father; at least not very much. His father had never hit him. In fact it was his mother who occasionally slapped his legs when he had a tantrum, but she never hurt more than his dignity and he knew she loved him. He wasn't so certain about his father. He thought Dad tried to love him but never quite succeeded.

His door opened and he jumped.

'It's not Dad, it's me,' his sister Georgie said. 'Don't

worry about him. He won't come. He's talking to Mum. Very seriously. What have you done now?'

'He's cross because I cried. He says boys don't cry, but I do. I can't help it. Tears just come out. I don't know how to stop them, Georgie. What can I do?'

Georgina smiled and hugged him. She was his favourite sister, a warm girl with soft brown eyes and freckles on her nose. 'You cry all you like, Harry. Dad's wrong. Boys do cry. And those who don't, should. Better than hitting people. Like Marcus does.'

'Does Dad hit people?' Harry asked nervously.

'No. No, he doesn't. He's not so bad, really, I suppose,' she added generously, 'but he's terribly old-fashioned. Mum says he's positively Victorian. And he expects too much. That's his trouble. Do you know what he said when I won my siver medal?'

'No. What?'

'He said, "Bad luck, Georgie. Never mind, you bring me back the gold next year." Bad luck! I'd been delighted with the silver. Ecstatic! When he said that, I could've thrown it at him.'

'I wish you had.'

There were footsteps on the stairs and his three other sisters came in.

'Oh, there you are,' Victoria said. 'You are a little mutt, Harry. Crying because you've lost a few curls! They'll grow again, silly. Now you've gone and put Dad in a bad mood for the rest of the day just when I wanted to borrow some money from him.'

'It wasn't because of my curls. I don't care about them.'

'Why was it, then?'

Harry couldn't explain. It had been the expression in his father's face when he'd seen the short hair. The pleased way he'd said, 'Ah, that's better. Now you look like a proper boy.' Harry knew what his father had meant by a proper boy. He meant a boy like Marcus, a boy who enjoyed riding tall horses with big yellow teeth. A boy who liked to play cricket with a hard ball that left bruises, and would sail with his father in a small boat on a rough, stomach-shaking sea, without being sick. Harry didn't think he could be that sort of boy. He didn't quite know what sort of boy he wanted to be, but he wished his dad would leave him to choose for himself.

'He says he can't help it,' Georgina told her sisters. 'He's only six. Didn't you ever cry when you were small, Vicky?'

'I don't think so. I don't remember,' Victoria replied. 'I think I was always tough.'

'I cried,' Julie said. 'I remember it well. My nose ran and Dad told me to wipe it. He said I looked disgusting with snot all over my face, so I decided to give up crying for ever.' She looked at herself in the mirror and smiled at her reflection. She was the prettiest of Harry's sisters, with hair as long and curly as his had been before it was cut.

'How?' he asked.

'How what? Oh, you mean, how did I stop myself crying? Let me see. I started by biting my lip, sometimes so hard it bled.'

'Didn't that make you cry more?'

'No. It sort of distracts your attention from what you were crying about. Then someone says, "Your lip's bleeding" and you say, "Oh is it really?" as if you hadn't noticed, and by the time you've finished talking about it, you've forgotten what you were crying about, see?'

'Mmmm,' Harry said doubtfully.

'Well, you try it,' Julie said kindly. 'I'll help you. And I'll teach you how to turn somersaults, if you like. Nothing like somersaults for cheering you up.'

'I'll help you too,' Georgie offered. 'I'll teach you to swim. In warm water,' she added, seeing he did not look any too pleased. 'It's lovely, honestly, Harry. And everyone has a wet face when they're swimming. Dad won't even notice if you cry.'

'And I'll lend you my gun,' said Nell, not to be outdone, though what she meant him to do with it, Harry wasn't sure. She was a silly girl.

'You're mad, all of you,' Victoria told her sisters. 'Somersaults and swimming and a gun! Supposing he wants to cry in the middle of the High Street? What's he to do then? All this fuss over Harry. Nobody bothered about us. We had to learn to swim at school, like everyone else. Nobody taught us to turn somersaults. We just copied the other kids. Dad was mean to us. He wouldn't even let me have riding lessons,' she added with an old bitterness, 'he said he couldn't afford it. But Harry! He can afford them for Harry. Harry can have everything he wants.'

'I don't want riding lessons. I don't think I like horses,' Harry explained.

'You're an idiot. You don't have to like them to sit on them,' Victoria told him scornfully. She turned to her sisters. 'You can't teach him anything. He's just a little coward. I'm not going to waste my time on him.'

Georgie told her she was mean, and Julie said it was just as well Vicky refused to help Harry, since she was a bully like Marcus, and would only make things worse. Nell said that Marcus had stepped on her china cat and broken it, and if Vicky broke anything of hers, she'd shoot her with her toy gun. They started quarrelling so loudly that Harry got into his bed, put his fingers in his ears, and waited for them to go away.

By the time they'd finished their quarrel, he was fast asleep. When they looked down at him, seeing his short, shaven head and the tear stains still streaking his flushed cheeks, even Victoria said softly, 'Poor little squirt,' and they agreed they would all help him and teach him what they could, and stop him being bullied at school.

Over the years Harry learned to hide his tears from his father. He learned to swim, though he never won any sort of medal. He rode an overlarge horse and fell off several times, breaking his collarbone twice and his arm once, and bit his lip till it bled but did not cry.

'Brave lad,' his father said, but added rather sadly, when Harry fell off once again, 'I don't think riding is your thing, is it, Harry? Perhaps we'd better give it up. I don't want you to break your neck. At least we tried.'

'The saddle is so slippery,' Harry apologised. 'Mum says I'd do better on a camel.'

'*A camel*?'

'She says they have cloth saddles like rugs, and a big pommel in front to hold on to with both hands,' Harry explained.

'How on earth does she know?'

'She was a teacher once, Dad,' Harry said, surprised that his father seemed to have forgotten.

'I know that, you silly boy,' his father said impatiently, 'but I've never heard that they teach camel riding in English schools.' He looked sideways at his son and added, 'I could try and find out for you if you wish, but I don't think you'd like it, Harry. Camels are a lot higher off the ground than horses.'

Harry flushed, realising then that for all his and his sisters' efforts, his father still knew he was a coward. He felt almost sorry for him, having such a disappointing son.

'Vicky loves horses, Dad,' he said. 'And she's very brave. She can ride, you know. She's practised on her friends' pony. But it's too small for her really. I'm sure she'd love to have proper lessons.'

It was his father's turn to flush. 'Yes. Yes. She did say something about it once, years ago, but we were hard up then. I couldn't afford it. I suppose I should have thought of it later, but somehow . . . Well, she can have lessons instead of you, if she likes. Your mother can drive her over –'

'I think she'd rather you did, Dad.'

'Oh you do, do you? Has your sister put you up to this?'

'No, Dad!'

'If she really wants riding lessons, she'll accept a lift from me or your mother, just as it suits us. Or go by bus, if we're both too busy. And you can tell her that. The idea! Putting down conditions –'

'She didn't, Dad. She doesn't know anything about it. It was my idea.'

His father snorted but said no more until they got home. Then he said, 'You can tell Victoria to let me know when she can go for lessons and I'll fix it up with the stables.'

'Thank you, Dad.'

Victoria was delighted when he told her. 'But did he actually say he wanted me to come in your place or was that your idea? No, don't bother to lie. I can see from your face he didn't even think of me.'

She looked so cross that for a moment he was afraid she was going to swear and shout and refuse to have any lessons, but then she tossed her head. 'I don't care! Stupid old Dad, as long as he pays for my lessons, I'll take them and be glad.' She put her arm round Harry and hugged him. 'You're a good kid.'

Harry smiled.

Harry hated sailing. Georgie had taught him to swim but could not teach him how not to be seasick in a small boat. 'You'll get over it in time,' Dad said, but Harry did not.

Now the holidays had begun, and Vicky and Georgie were back home from college, his father was still determined to teach Harry to sail.

'You should take one of those pills I gave you,' he said impatiently the next time they were out on the choppy sea. 'You're beginning to look green again.'

'I tried one last week but it didn't work. In fact, it made me feel worse.'

His father was silent for a moment; then he said, 'Perhaps if I took you out for a long trip, a week or two, it might cure you once and for all.'

Harry didn't answer. He couldn't. He was hanging over the side of the boat being horribly sick. His father sighed, and pushing the tiller round, made for the shore. As they were walking home, he looked down at his son. The boy was not crying, but his face was as white as cuttlefish. He looked utterly miserable.

'Oh, all right, Harry,' his father said with rough

ᴉness, 'I won't take you out again. It obviously isn't your thing.'

'Sorry, Dad.'

'Not your fault.'

Harry glanced at his father. Perhaps this was the right time to ask. He opened his mouth . . .

'What is it, Harry?' his father asked. 'You look just like a fish. Speak up, boy, if there's something you want to say. Otherwise shut your mouth.'

'It's just . . . Georgie would like to go sailing, Dad, and I'm sure she'd not be sick. She loves anything to do with water. Remember all those medals she's won for swimming in the county championships –'

'Yes, indeed. How many is it now? Five silvers and one bronze?'

'Not everyone can win the gold!' Harry said hotly.

'No. of course not.' His father sounded surprised, having forgotten the unlucky remark that had so offended Georgina in the past. 'Oh well. Tell Georgina she can come sailing with me instead of you.' He was silent for a moment. Then he looked down at Harry and added, 'You're quite clever in your way, aren't you, Harry? What about Julie? Are you going to tell me she's longing to play cricket with me? And Nell wants to come to football matches with me? And all the other things you do with me only because you're too frightened to refuse? Are you really so scared of me that you can't say straight out, "No thank you, Dad"?'

Harry flushed, the bright colour flooding his pale face. There were times when he almost hated his father.

'I'm not scared of you, Dad,' he said angrily. 'I'm sorry for you.'

'*You* are sorry for *me*?'

'Yes, I am,' Harry said, stung by the contempt in his father's voice.

'Do you mind telling me why?'

'Because you're never happy, that's why! You always want something you haven't got. Like a gold medal from Georgie when she's just won the silver. Like a boy from Mum when she's just given you a girl. Four girls! I bet every time you saw the next one, you didn't even smile. How do you think that made them feel? Didn't you care? And then when you have a son at last, it isn't the right sort. Oh no, you wanted a son like Marcus. But all you got was me. Tough luck.'

His father's face was as red as fire, but when he spoke, his voice was cold. 'Have you quite finished, Harry?'

Might as well be hung for a sheep as a lamb, Harry thought.

'No. I want to say I'm sorry for Uncle William, too.'

'And what has he done to displease you?'

'He had a son like Marcus, that's what. How you can prefer him to me, I don't know. It's – it's an insult!' Harry shouted. 'I wouldn't have minded so much if he'd been a decent sort of boy, but he's not. He's horrible!'

For a long time his father did not say anything. His mouth was tightly shut as if he was afraid to open it in case he exploded.

I've done it now, thought Harry.

They walked towards the car park in silence. For all its disadvantages, Harry was used to being his father's favourite child. It made a special bond between them, even though at times the bond was more like a chain.

At last, his father said quietly, 'Try not to be envious of your cousin just because he is more successful than you.'

'Not at everything! Only at sport and not even all sports, either. I can run faster than he can. Much faster.'

'I expect you've had a lot of practice running away,' his father said.

Later, when they were driving home, he apologised as he usually did when he thought he'd hurt Harry's feelings. 'I'm sorry. That was an unkind thing to say. It's not your fault. I know you try hard. Don't think I haven't noticed.'

Harry did not answer.

The next morning was warm and sunny. He found three of his sisters in the garden. Georgie was painting her toenails green to match the grass. Victoria was sitting on a wooden chair, shelling some broad beans for their mother, and Julie was standing on her head, showing off. Nell was spending the day with a school friend.

'Hullo, Harry,' Georgie said. 'Are you at a loose end,

too? It's only the third week of our holidays and I've nothing better to do than paint my toenails. Do you like them?'

'Yes, but you should have painted them sea-green, not grass-green,' he said. 'Dad wants you to go sailing with him on Saturday. He asked me to tell you.'

'What? But he's always said that the boat won't hold more than two.'

'I won't be going.'

Julie came down from her headstand and sat cross-legged on the grass. They all stared at him.

'Something's happened, hasn't it?' Georgie said. 'I thought you looked a bit off colour last night. Have you had a row with Dad?'

'I was sick again. I'm sure he thinks I do it to annoy him.'

'He can't really. If he said so, it was probably his idea of a joke,' Victoria said. 'You know how clumsy he can be, always offending people. But he can be jolly nice when you get to know him. Since I've been riding with him, I've got to like him a lot. He's really quite different . . . You go sailing with him, Georgie.'

'I don't think I'd better. I might be tempted to push him overboard.'

Harry knew she really wanted to go, and said quickly, 'No, you won't. You'll enjoy it. And I'll try and think of something for Julie –'

'Don't bother!' Julie cried. 'I'm not doing anything

boring just to get to know Dad better. Besides, I already get on quite well with him as it is.'

'That's because you're his idea of a proper girl,' Harry said. 'You're pretty and fluffy –'

'And vain,' said Georgie.

'And silly,' Vicky added.

'And you're all just jealous,' Julie said, not in the least put out by this. 'You know, Dad thinks gymnastics are like dancing lessons for little girls. He's no idea what a hard discipline it is.'

'Why don't you invite him to see your next show at school?' Harry suggested.

'He wouldn't come. He'd find something to be too busy with. You know what's he's like.'

'I think I can get him to come,' Victoria said slowly. 'He's changing a bit. He listens more. He's nicer. What have you been doing to him, Harry?'

'Educating Dad, that's my plan,' Harry said, and laughed. 'I'm trying to teach him to appreciate his daughters. I've given up trying to teach him to appreciate his son.'

'Harry! Don't say that!'

'It's all right. I feel wonderful! I feel free! I'm not going to try and be what Dad wants any longer. I'm not going to go into the boring family business when I leave school. A chain of butchers' shops – can you see me going round the country counting sausages? I'm practically a vegetarian. From now on, I'm going to be me and do what suits me.'

'And what's that?' they asked.

'I don't know,' he said and laughed with them. 'Isn't it wonderful?' He flung his arms up into the sunny air. 'I can be anything. Anything at all. I feel like turning cartwheels and somersaults in the air! I'm free as a bird!'

Harry had grown into a tall, amiable boy, and was well-liked at school. He knew his mother and his sisters loved him, and for a while he thought that was enough. He was a member of the Riverside Harriers and ran for his school. He had learned to play the trumpet and sing the latest songs. He could speak French and Italian fairly well and was going on a walking tour on the continent with his friends next year.

And yet there was a hole in his life, an empty space around the edges of which his father walked politely, like a stern, silent ghost. Never shouting, never losing his temper, never asking for his company.

'How is he?' Harry sometimes asked his sisters, who knew Dad better now than he did.

'He's fine,' they said, and they added, looking at him sideways, 'but he misses you.'

'Oh yeah? Why doesn't he ask me out somewhere then?'

'You know how proud he is. He'd be afraid of losing face –'

What about my face? Harry thought. But his face was

young, he could afford to lose a bit of it here and there. It would grow again.

But did he really want to put himself back into bondage to his father, now that he was free? Oddly enough, the answer was yes. He too had changed. He was old enough and strong enough to resist the weight of his father's ambitions for him, and go his own way. All his life Harry had wanted his father to admire him. It was a dream he couldn't give up. So when the local teams started playing football again in the park, he asked his father if he'd like to come and watch.

At first he thought his father was not going to answer. But then he said, 'I thought you didn't like watching football with me, Harry.'

'That was cricket. I do like football.'

'Then let's go,' said his father, smiling at him. 'By all means, let's go.'

They went nearly every week and enjoyed themselves. One day his father asked Harry to come to the Cup Final with him. 'I have two tickets,' he told him, smiling.

Harry was surprised. 'But Dad, don't you usually take Marcus?'

'That boy!' his father said, in a tone of voice that made Harry's heart sing. 'I've been gravely disappointed in your cousin Marcus. I've been hearing things about him, very unpleasant things . . . Not that I'd believe mere gossip, of course, but it made me watch him carefully myself. I tell you, Harry, that boy's a lout and a bully. I saw him with my own eyes twist your sister Nell's arm, and laugh when she cried! And when I told him what I thought of him, he refused to apologise. He called me an old – well, never mind what he said. I never thought to hear such language from him. I'm sorry for my poor brother having such a son. You were right. You never liked him, did you?'

'No,' Harry agreed happily.

'I find that neither your mother nor your sisters liked him either; I was the only one who was blind. However, my eyes are open now. You are the boy a father can be proud of. Not Marcus, but you.'

The Old Team

Helen Dunmore

My brother Adam sits by the window, staring out, staring at nothing.

'I've got some calls to make in Nether Sowden. Why don't you come along, Adam? I'd be glad of the company,' says Dad, in the deliberately cheerful voice he uses all the time with Adam now. Adam turns away from the window and frowns, looking at Dad. His hands are curled into fists.

'Can't you leave me alone?'

'I was only asking –'

'I know. I know you were only asking. *But I don't want to come.*'

He gets up and walks heavily out of the room. We hear his feet clumping upstairs, back to the attic where he spends most of his time now.

'What does he do up there all day?' Dad asks me.

'He reads,' I say, though I know Adam doesn't read. He sits in a fog of silence, and I can't find a way through it.

'Brooding,' says Dad. 'That won't do him any good. He ought to get out and about. It'd take him out of himself.' Dad rubs his face hard with the backs of his hands, as if he's trying to rub something away. 'You can't expect him to be just as he was,' he goes on. 'It'll take time. Don't say anything to your mother.' He goes out of the room too, and I hear the creak of the stairs. Is he going up after Adam? I wish he would. Dad's a doctor, he ought to be able to help somehow. Then he stops. After a while his footsteps come down, go across the hall, and out to the garden.

You can't expect him to be just as he was. I know that. I know how lucky we are that he's here at all. I've got my brother here at home, not like Danny Forrester, or Tony Loblow. Sometimes I think about what would have happened if Adam hadn't been wounded in March. A Blighty one, that's what it's called: a wound that was serious enough to get him sent home, but not bad enough to kill him.

The Germans started their big advance on 21st March. If Adam hadn't been wounded, he'd have been in the worst of the fighting. Half the battalion was killed, he told me. Doesn't Dad know that? Bannerman's dead. Bannerman used to get more parcels from home than anyone. He used to get roast chicken and fruitcake and wine and tinned oysters. He always shared them out. 'Dig in before the rats get it,' he said. Adam told me that. He told me about Oliver, who kept a pet mouse which ate everything except cheese. I wonder if the mouse escaped, or if he's dead too? Adam's best friend in the company was Carter. Carter was going to come and stay with us on his next home leave. He was going to teach me to play the mouth organ.

Adam talks to me, a bit. He told me about Carter being killed by a shell, then he said, 'I should have been with them.'

'But you were wounded, Adam,' I said. 'You couldn't have fought like that.'

Adam wouldn't listen. 'I should have been there,' he repeated. 'You don't know what it's like, Bart. If I hadn't got this shrapnel in my shoulder –'

'If you hadn't got shrapnel in your shoulder you'd be dead, too,' I said. I was angry. It sounded as if he didn't want to come back to us. As if he didn't even want to be alive.

Two years ago Adam was on home leave before he went out to the front in France. So many men had gone from our village already. On Sundays the church had a lopsided look, full of women and children. Adam told me how Mrs Quignall had asked him to take a message to Sam, even though Adam was in a different battalion and wouldn't be in the same sector of the front. She'd got a medal for Sam to wear around his neck. It was supposed to have the power to stop a bullet. Adam weighed the medal in his hand.

'Will you take it?' I asked.

'Course I will,' Adam said. 'You never know, I might meet up with some of the old team out there.' He meant the cricket team, the team he'd played for every summer since he was fourteen. He smiled, and said, 'What do you bet old Georgie's bowling fast ones to those Jerries, Bart?'

I smiled, but I was frightened. I didn't want Adam to go to France, even though I knew he had to. There wasn't any other way. The war had already been going on for two years. At the beginning everyone thought it would be over in a few months, but now it seemed as if it could go on for ever. There didn't seem to be any reason for it to stop. There would be more and more littl'uns wearing black armbands, more and more women dressed in black, and fewer and fewer men.

Adam's wound is healing. He was wounded in the right shoulder, but he's left-handed. He could still play cricket if he wanted to. But whenever I ask if he'll come out and bowl for me, he just says, 'Where's the use? The team's all gone.' *Jem Forrester, Mikey Loblow, Sam Quignall, Jackie* and *Budge Linklater, Georgie Low, Tom Low, Paul Quick.* And all the others.

Georgie Low got hit by shrapnel too, but much worse than Adam. His wound went gangrenous and he had to have his leg cut off. He sits in a cane chair in the kitchen all day long. He can still feel his leg, even though it's not there. His father came up to our house to talk to my father.

You could hear old Low all over the house. He's the blacksmith, and you have to yell out to make yourself heard in the forge. Georgie Low was going to be a blacksmith, too, but you can't be a blacksmith with one leg.

'He still feels his leg, see, Doctor, like it's as real as yours or mine. He cries out at night when it pains him. Can't you give him something for it?'

Then Dad talked to old Low for a long time, but I couldn't hear what he was saying. I went out into the garden, chalked a wicket on the stable wall, and practised my bowling. My action was getting a lot better. After a while Dad came out and walked up and down the lawn, his head bent. I wished he'd come over and watch me, but he didn't. I thought he was going to walk straight past me, but then he stopped, put his hand on my shoulder and said, 'Thank God you're only thirteen, Bart.'

I'm only thirteen. I won't be going to the war, not unless it goes on for twenty years like some people say it will. It's July 1918, and the war has lasted for four years already. Now it's summer again, bright and hot like the summer the war began. That was the year our team won the Sowden Downs Villages Cup. A man came and took a photograph of the team, most of them standing, some sitting cross-legged on the grass. Timmy Ripley reckoned he'd got a wasp in his trousers and it took the photographer half-an-hour to get enough order to take the picture. Timmy's still out in France. His ma had a field postcard from him last week.

There they all are in the photograph, Adam in the middle holding the Cup, Georgie Low frowning because the sun was in his eyes, standing there with his arms folded. Georgie Low was our best fast bowler. He used to come up to the house every day in the summer holidays, when Adam was home from school, and they'd practise on the pitch we'd made in the old orchard.

'Can't we cut down some of the trees, Dad?' Adam had begged. 'Those apples are all maggots anyway. The trees'll make good firewood.' And in the end Dad had agreed. A couple of men came up from the village, chopped down the trees and grubbed up the stumps.

Once the long grass was scythed, we had a decent pitch. I was only six then, so Adam must have been going on fifteen. I got sent to bed at seven o'clock, and I used to hang out of the window in the long light evenings, listening to the ball cracking against the bat, and the shouts of Jem Forrester, Mikey Loblow, Sam Quignall, Jackie and Budge Linklater, the Low boys. I couldn't wait till I was big enough to join in. Sometimes they used to let me field, and when no one else was there Adam would put me in front of the stumps, and bowl to me. He was teaching me to bowl as well, and when he was away at school I'd practise for hours against the stable wall, because that was what Adam had told me to do.

'You'll never be any good if you don't practise, Bart.'

I practised all right. Hour after hour, on my own but never lonely, thinking about what Adam would say when he came home on holiday and saw how hard I'd worked to improve. Sometimes I could almost hear him: 'You're coming on, Bart,' he'd say.

Jem Forrester's dead. Mikey Loblow's still out in France, like Timmy. Sam Quignall, Jackie and Budge Linklater, Tom Low, they're all dead. Sam was killed in training when a grenade went off in his hand. That's not what they said in the official letter, but Joe Farnell from Over Sowden was there and he saw what happened. He never told Mrs Low. Better for her to think he died fighting, but some of us know. Jackie and Budge are missing, believed killed. Tom died of wounds in April this year.

So there isn't any cricket team any more. There's plenty of littl'uns in the village who've never seen a decent game. The boys my age can remember what it was like when the village cricket field used to be mowed and rolled ready for Saturday. They only mowed a rectangle: the outfield was pasture, and you were lucky if there were sheep grazing on it, not cattle. Adam used to tell me about finding the ball deep in a cowpat when he was fielding. It's all long grass now, rough and tangled. You can't imagine playing cricket on it.

The visiting teams came from Over Sowden and Nether Sowden and all around. There was tea in the Village Hall – bread and jam and fruit loaf and iced fancies – and then afterwards there was beer in the *Crossed Hands* all night. The visitors would go wobbling off on their bikes, and then our team walked home in the dark, singing and swaying. Most times I'd be sent off home long before the night was over, but I remember once they let me stay, squeezed in between Jackie and Budge. Everywhere there were red faces roaring out songs and jokes I didn't really understand, but I laughed anyway, and I drank beer out of Budge's glass when he let me. All I wanted was to be with them. One day I'd *be* them, one of the team, sunburnt and sweating, squinting my eyes against the sun.

It's July 1918. The team's gone, cricket's finished. That's what everyone in the village is saying, even when they don't open their mouths. There aren't any laughing faces in the *Crossed Hands* any more. Only old men. The black armbands say it's all over. Everything's over except the war, which will still be going on when everything else is dead. Adam's face says it too, when he sits staring at nothing. But I look down at my hand, grasping the cricket ball, feeling its smooth leather weight. I could drop the ball on the ground and walk away, but I don't want to. I want to bowl. I want to bat. I'm a fair batsman, a middling-to-good bowler, and not a bad fielder. A good all-rounder, that's what I want to be. I want to be better and faster. I want to learn everything I can. I need to learn now. It's not all over for me: it hasn't even begun. And I want my brother back.

I've got a plan. It's three summers since Dad last had

the pitch in the orchard scythed and rolled. The grass is long and tussocky, nearly as bad as the village cricket field. Hens get out of the henhouses and lay their eggs down there. You wouldn't believe that Adam and Georgie and the others used to play there. Dad didn't think it was worth bothering to keep the pitch, just for me. That's what he said, anyway. *When you're older, Bart. With the war, I can't get the men to do the work.* But I knew there was another reason. He didn't want to hear the sound of the ball clocking against the bat, or voices shouting in the orchard. Not while Adam was in France, in danger of dying every day. Not while telegrams were coming for the Lows, the Quignalls and the Linklaters. He wanted the grass to grow long and cover up everything.

But I'm not going to let him. It's no use asking him, so I'm going to do it myself. I'm not the only one. Danny Forrester'd play, so would Tony Loblow, and maybe Jake Martin, and there's others, littl'uns as well as the boys my age. We ought to be learning. *It's our turn.*

Tiny Metcham says he'll come up and scythe, after he finishes his work. He wants a shilling for it. He's six foot in his stockinged feet, and he says he's still the strongest man in the village, even though he's fifty-seven.

I asked Arthur Loblow about the roller (he's Mikey and Tony's grandad). 'It'll want greasing,' he says. 'You'll never move it. It takes a strong man.' Tony answered that me and him and Danny add up to a strong man, and then his

82

grandad said if we thought we could do it, then good luck to us. He wasn't going to stand in our way.

Tiny Metcham found a nest with six eggs in it. Hen's eggs, speckled brown. He lifted the eggs up carefully and put them in his cap.

'You give these to your ma,' he said. 'Daft creature, laying away. Well, not so daft mebbe. It's nature to want to rear your own young 'uns, and keep a hold on 'em.'

I watch the scything, and I carry away armfuls of the fallen grass and spread them out to dry. It's quiet in the orchard, away from the house, hidden by the hedges. There's only the hiss of the scythe through swathes of grass, and the rasp when Tiny sharpens its blade on the whetstone. The pitch starts to appear, pale and shorn, bumpy with molehills. I measure it out. All the time I keep looking towards the house in case anyone comes, but no one does. I pay Tiny his shilling, and he thanks me and asks after Adam.

' 'Spect we'll be seeing him down the *Crossed Hands* one of these nights. He'll have to be getting his cricket boots on.'

'Yes,' I say.

Getting the roller up to the orchard is the worst job. Even with the three of us wrestling, it's a brute to move. First of all we spend hours sandpapering the rust off the rollers, and oiling it. It makes you want to kick it, it's so huge and heavy and filthy. It's been lying in a shed for three years. Tony and Danny and I swear as we shove and shoulder it out onto the lane. We're out of breath and sweating already. But we said we'd do it, and we're *going* to do it. I don't care who sees us now. If my dad does, I'd tell him what we're doing. Nothing's going to stop us.

We drag the roller up onto the newly-shorn pitch. My back hurts and there's sweat and streaks of black on our faces. Jake Martin saw us, and came to join in. He reckons his dad has a set of pads put away we could use. I don't want to ask Dad, or Adam: not yet.

Back and forth we stumble, all of us shoving at the roller handle, over molehills and ruts and tussocks, flattening them down. As we make a turn I think I catch a glimpse of something moving behind the hedge. I squint against the sun, which is sinking towards evening, but whoever it was, they've gone. As long as they don't stop us. Not now.

It's nearly dark when Tony says, 'Won't get it much more level than this.'

And we won't. It's not perfect, but it never was. It's good enough. Jake positions himself where the crease might be, and swipes with an imaginary bat.

'Coming up tomorrow then?' I ask, and they all nod.

'We going to let the littl'uns come up?' asks Danny.

'We're going to need them,' I say. 'If we're ever going to get a team.'

It's hard to sleep. Adam's going to know tomorrow. As soon as he hears the sound of the bat on the ball, and the voices, he'll know something's going on. And then what? I've planned it so far, but what's going to happen now? My mind races, while the smell of cut grass drifts in through my wide-open window. I wonder if Adam can smell it too.

After breakfast I go straight down to the orchard. Danny and Jake and Tony are there already, and they've brought a couple of littl'uns with them – the Harborne twins.

'You want to bat, Bart?' offers Jake.

'No, we'll put Tony in first, you, Danny, then me. Either of you littl'uns want to try? All right, Bertie next, then Al in last.'

I want to see what they can do. Same with the bowling. This is the start of building up the team. Al Harborne goes behind the wicket ('He's little, but he's tough,' says Tony), with Jake at long stop. Tony batting, Danny to bowl. I'm in the outfield, along with Bertie. The grass is almost up to Bertie's waist, but he's sharp-eyed and he swoops down on the ball when it rolls behind a patch of thistles.

Danny's not a bad bowler; at least he's accurate. Tony's strong, and he places his bat squarely to the ball. He hits a few singles off Danny's bowling, then we change over. They're warming up, getting going. Bertie throws well, and then he muffs an easy catch and his twin jeers. Bertie's face darkens. He makes for Al, but I haul him back. All the Harbornes are famous for fighting.

'You want to be in this team or not? And belt up, Al. This is a *practice*.'

I don't think about anything but the next ball. I don't notice the sound of the bat on the ball, or our shouts, or the way the noise carries. I don't hear footsteps, or see a shape moving behind the hedge. I don't see anything, and then I look up and there he is. My brother Adam, inside the orchard hedge, watching us. He stands there with his arms folded, like Georgie Low in that old photograph.

Tony's bowling now, to Jake. Tony runs up. Good action, nice ball. But Jake's seen Adam. His concentration vanishes, he fumbles trying to play a defensive shot, and he's clean-bowled.

I wave to Adam. He lifts his hand in a salute.

'I heard you,' he says. 'Thought I'd come down. Good game?'

'It's just a practice,' I say.

'You've got the old pitch in good shape,' says Adam.

'It's still pretty rough. It hasn't been used since –'

'I know,' says Adam. 'Carry on. Don't let me stop you.'

I hesitate. 'Do you want to –'

'I'll just watch,' says Adam.

This time Danny's batting. He's the best so far. He swipes the ball into the stinging nettles and gets two runs off it. Things are starting to take shape. Danny's back at the wicket. Then I look at Adam and for a second I forget everything. I don't watch the ball, or Danny, or any of them. I see what Adam sees. I see a different sun shining, casting different shadows. I see Jem Forrester running up, and then Jackie Linklater leaping for the catch off Sam's bat. I hear the clock of the ball, and Jackie's yell. Sun streams in their faces, and their shirts stick to their backs with sweat. This is *their* place, and it always will be.

Then they vanish, and there's only Adam, staring across at me.

'What are you playing at? You missed that catch,' he says.

'I was –'

'You were woolgathering,' he says. 'You can't do that. Not when you're playing cricket.'

'So were you,' I say.

The practice has stopped. The others are looking at us, curious and uneasy.

'Get back to it,' says Adam. 'You were doing fine.'

'How long've you been watching?'

'Long enough.'

'You reckon you could come down and coach us some time?'

We're all looking at him now, hoping. At last, slowly, he says, 'I'm not doing the work for you. It's *your* team. But I'll coach if you like, when I can. I'm not going to be here long, Bart. You know that.'

And I find I do. Adam's got to have a different life, and

it can't be here, where there are ghosts for him on every patch of ground.

'All right,' I say. 'Tomorrow?'

'Tomorrow.' Adam nods, and turns to walk up to the orchard gate.

As I watch him go, I see them again. Budge and Jackie, Mikey and Jem, Paul Quick, Sam Quignall. They close in around my brother. They walk away together, arms round one another's shoulders, the light of the evening sun catching the backs of their heads. And then they are gone, and I know I'll never see them again.

I turn back to my team.

Someone Else's Father

Julie Myerson

It was the hottest summer in ten years and we had a new father. His name was Colin Finch but we'd always called him Uncle Colin and Mum said there was no reason at all why that should change.

He was no relation to us. In fact, he was still someone else's husband. Auntie Sandra's. But they were getting a divorce and when it came, there'd be a party and Mum would be the new Mrs Finch. And we'd all have new outfits and possibly even go on the honeymoon with them.

Actually, Uncle Colin wasn't just someone else's husband. He was also someone else's father. Everyone knew he'd left his two boys to be with us – swapped sons for daughters, and that big white farmhouse complete with a dovecot for a mouldy brick terrace in the city centre. But anyone could see why he'd chosen Mum (thin, pretty, glittery eyeshadow) over Auntie Sandra (brown-haired and churchy). It just seemed a shame that his two lads had to lose out.

Ian was my age – serious and quite nice-looking, catching the bus home with his battered leather bag with the stickers all peeling off. Mike was only seven with sticky-out ears and a handbag tied to his tricycle handlebars. We all thought he was sweet. I didn't like to think of them waking up one morning and hey presto, no dad. What would they be told? What would they think?

Would they be all alone at the breakfast table with Auntie Sandra, while we sat and stared at Uncle Colin who'd come in the night with as many of his things as he could cram in the back of his Rover? There wasn't much – just a load of antiquey things that didn't work any more. But I liked his dog, Twigs, who trembled all over when I bent to stroke her. 'She's always like that,' Uncle Colin said, 'trembly. That's whippets for you. It's the breed.'

So Twigs crouched quivering in a corner and we had a kind of celebration breakfast. Normally we just had cereal, but today there was toast with the two-tone chocolate spread that Mum kept in the cupboard for birthdays. Normally we begged for it, but today it was hard to get excited.

'To us!' said Uncle Colin and he raised his coffee cup in a pathetic way that made my sister burst into tears. Mum balanced her cigarette on her saucer and pulled Liddy onto her lap.

'Tired,' she mouthed at Uncle Colin. And then she cocked her head on one side in the way she'd read that top models do when they're being photographed. This is life, Mum! I wanted to shout at her, there's no camera here!

'I'm not tired,' Liddy snarled, but of course they totally ignored her.

'Hello? Liddy just spoke to you?' I told Mum crossly.

'I heard,' she said, and smiled at me with her eyes all crinkled up as if all of this was normal. She had a silk scarf tied around her ponytail and you could tell she was embarrassed because she knew that we knew that Uncle Colin had slept in the same double bed with her all night long.

Our dad really hated Uncle Colin. Since our mum left him, he'd hated everyone and everything. He said Uncle Colin had broken up two marriages. A Homebreaker, he called him, which made you think of some kind of lunatic with a mallet, instead of just an ordinary chartered surveyor.

Dad was jealous of course. Because he was a cross, going-bald man in a cardigan, who didn't have a wife any more and didn't have a clue about housework. Our old house – where he still lived – was a total fiasco without Mum. It made me sad to see the cobwebs on the stairs and the brown stains in the sink and smell the damp unlovedness of that place.

When I slept there, in my old room, I sometimes woke

in the night and was afraid to open my eyes because of all the neglect around me. It was spooky, that neglect. It made you think someone could die there and no one would ever find them.

I was secretly glad no one sided with Dad, who was mean as mustard and should never have married. He pretended to slow down for hitchhikers and then tore off again as soon as they picked up their bags. He liked to invite Jehovah's Witnesses into the house just to make them sweat. He made us late for school for the same reason.

And I was glad we'd got Uncle Colin, even if he did belong to someone else. He was like a father out of a book, with his film star face and going-out shirt with the ruffles down the front. He liked poems and golf and anything to do with the war, and he had certificates for everything he'd ever done. And records of the Grenadier Guards playing 'Lovely Boating Weather'.

I asked Uncle Colin about life and everything and he said he thought he sort of believed in God. Or if not God, then Something. That made me think, because our father had always said religion was for wimps. But it didn't seem unmanly at all when Uncle Colin talked about it.

Eventually Twigs missed Auntie Sandra too much and had to go back to her. Uncle Colin was sad, but he said it wasn't fair on the dog. I liked the way he put the dog's feelings first. He had a bit of a double chin when he was upset or sorry for someone or if you looked at him from the wrong angle. Sometimes he took little red pills for blood pressure.

But he was such fun! He could grasp Liddy by the wrist and ankle and spin her round till she spluttered and choked. He did a game where you were blindfolded and he dressed up as a pirate and said 'Feel my eye' and mashed your finger – spludge! – into an eggcup of jelly. He knew the names of birds and he taught us rounds to sing in the car.

And, unlike Dad, who never travelled more than ten miles from his home if he could help it, Uncle Colin was well acquainted with the whole of the British Isles and could find his way around an Ordnance Survey map. He took us up mountains and showed us tumuli. He bought us cream teas. He made us get up early and walk in the rain.

Finally, he said it was time we had a family holiday – all of us, the boys too. And without even consulting Mum, he went and bought a caravan.

We'd never stayed in one before. It was marvellous.

He got it from the Mart. The foam cushions smelled of instant potato and there was a chemical loo called a Portapotty, which Uncle Colin had to deal with. If you wanted to use it, you had to make sure you told everyone you were going or someone might come in on you. There was no lock, just a canvas curtain without a zip.

'It's all right for the young ones,' I said.

'Don't be silly,' Uncle Colin said. 'It's no different from the army.' I said I didn't know about that as I had no intention of going in the army. 'Quite right,' he said, as if I'd agreed with him all along, when I hadn't.

But I'd have died if Ian had found me there. I had to put off going till he had gone off on a walk or something. Ian and I hardly ever spoke, but sometimes I saw him listening really hard when I said things – and then if I caught his eye he quickly looked away, making a gap between us. Thinking about this gap and the way he ignored me harder than everyone else gave me a funny tight feeling in my stomach. Like a period pain only squeezier and slipperier.

It wasn't that I fancied him – I mean, he was about an inch shorter than me – but there was a fizzy connection, a current flashing and tripping between us. In the caravan we slept under an awning and our sleeping bags were bang next to each other. Through the zip-opening you could see the sprinkle of stars in the cold black triangle of sky. Ian's sleeping bag was dark green nylon and smelled of boy. This was a new smell to me – the smell of feet and silence and looking like you didn't care about things.

The caravan site was in a field next to a pub called 'The Snooty Fox'. And next to the pub was a jalopy race track. All day long the cars droned round and the dust flew up in clouds around the caravans whose doors had to be shut despite the heat.

'Just our luck,' laughed Mum, 'landing up next to a bloody racing track!'

But you could tell her jolliness was put on. She hated walking to the shower block carrying her soap and towel along with everyone else. She was already sick of things falling out of cupboards and all that dishing up Spam and Smash in such a cramped space.

When Mum left Dad, he said he would punish her.

'Whatever it takes,' he said, as he stirred the Heinz tomato soup with a metal spoon so that it jarred your fillings, 'I'll get her back. She thinks she's got away with it, but she came to me with nothing and I told her she'd leave with nothing. I'm going to make sure she ends up with nothing. And people are going to hear about what she's done to me, That Woman.'

That Woman. The way he said it, with his eyes gone dead and wafts of blueish cigarette smoke escaping from his mouth, was scary. I was scared of what he might have to do, to satisfy his anger. And you shouldn't have to be scared of your own father – most people's dads are there to protect them, to make things seem better, not worse. I had friends at school whose fathers took them out for pizza and bought them presents even though they were divorced.

Not mine. I think he quite wanted us to feel that

humpback bridge feeling in our stomachs, the sudden sick lurch when you're confused about what's going on. So as not to give in, I'd straightaway switch my brain over and think of other things: the punch lines of jokes, what I'd watched on TV last night, whippets and whether I could have one when I was 'a bit more responsible', as Mum loved to say.

Then my dad's voice would break in on my thoughts: You're smiling now, he'd go, but just you wait.

In the middle of the night, I felt a hand pressing on my mouth. Dad. I wanted to cry out, but all my body was weighed down with missing him and I couldn't move.

I tried to see Ian, who was sound asleep next to me, but all I saw was darkness, like when you try to look into the centre of a dream and find you've gone past it.

My heart was hurting and I began to cry. And Dad's face was there, above my head, only I realised there was something wrong with it and it was this: it was a young, kind, tired face, not the desperate, overflowing one he'd had lately.

'Dad,' I whispered, then, 'Daddy?'

He said nothing, but his cheeks were wet with crying. I felt a terrible tearing inside.

You're hurting me, I wanted to say, but even as I said it I could tell that our feelings were all mixed up and it might just as well have been me hurting him. Everything had gone so sad on us – even he didn't mean the bad things he'd said. He just wished for the old days back, and him and Mum laughing and kissing in the kitchen while the potatoes banged away in the steaming pan.

Then the dream turned – pzoom! – and we were on the road where we lived when I was about five, Dad and me, and I was on the tricycle I used to have then – the one I'd forgotten all about, with the Noddy bell and the squishy, dirty white tyres. And Dad was trotting along next to me with his hands in his pockets and you could hear the change jingling away in there, only slightly muffled by the big white and a bit used hanky which he always carried in with the money.

I was laughing and so was Dad and it must have been a long time ago because he didn't even have his bald patch, but he was wearing the beige cardigan which I do remember. Or maybe I just remember it from photos.

And I kept saying, 'Daddy!' because I was having such a nice time and he kept saying something back to me, only however hard I listened I couldn't quite manage to hear what it was.

Of course, I can't really remember going along on my tricycle with him like that. Which is why when I woke up from such a beautiful, wonderful dream, I was crying.

I must have been loud, because Ian leaned up on one arm blinking and flicked on his torch. It was the torch he used when he went badger watching.

'What?' he said.

'Nothing.'

'Bad dream?'

'Mmm.'

He lay down again and shut his eyes and then – oh God! – stretched out a hand. I felt its weight on my sleeping bag just where my spine ended and my bottom began. Ian!

I couldn't breathe and it was like I was still on the tricycle, wind lifting my hair. My blood was rushing round my body so fast it felt like it would all gush out.

He sighed and I sighed back.

'I don't have a girlfriend,' he whispered.

My heart banged in my ears.

I stretched out my hand and put it near his face, near his pillow and he took it. His lips touched my shaking wrist and I shivered.

Morning came like the end of a wonderful movie – too fast, too sudden, too loud. The crashing in my head had gathered shape – the awning was shuddering under the weight of all that pouring rain.

Mum unzipped the flap and dashed in from outside, her hair slicked back and soaking.

'What?' I sat up, pulling my hand from where it lay too near Ian's.

'Weather's broken, kids,' she said and she sounded

almost happy. She went into the caravan and shut the door and I heard her talking to Uncle Colin.

Ian was just waking up. He didn't look at me and I didn't look at him. I knew he wouldn't look at me all day and possibly not the day after that, but I didn't care. There was no need to say anything to anyone. There was no need to say anything to anyone ever again.

We ate cornflakes at the formica table, with the rain banging so loud and hard no one bothered to talk.

'It's been chucking it down since five,' said Mum as she piled dishes in the tiny sink.

She said it to no one in particular and no one replied.

'Next time,' she said, 'we're bringing paper plates.'

I was surprised she said 'next time', but her saying it made me feel we were a proper family now, with holidays and a future together – a string of dates and memories stretching ahead of us through time.

'And party cups!' said Mike.

'Yeah, and whistles,' laughed Uncle Colin, doing the thing of snipping at his nose and pretending it had come off in his fingers.

He was busy twiddling the knobs of the radio to catch the forecast. He was a proper traveller in that way – always catching the shipping forecast and the traffic news and all that stuff.

'OK,' he said at last, 'we're going home.'

Mum looked relieved.

He squeezed her hand on the table. 'Not much point in staying if it's not going to brighten up,' he said.

I looked at their two hands gripping each other there on the table. I hoped I hadn't gone red.

It was still drizzling as we packed up the car and Uncle Colin sorted the Portapotty and undid the awning, which took ages and had to be done with Allen keys and a hammer and screwdriver.

Ian and I put on our cagoules and Ian never looked at me, but when Uncle Colin asked if I could collect up the screws and I passed them to Ian, he brushed my wet fingers more than was necessary and that's all I needed to make me feel floaty with happiness.

We left before lunch. Uncle Colin said we'd stop for a ploughman's when we got on the road.

'What a lovely holiday!' said Mum, who obviously couldn't wait to get back to her own bathroom and electric cooker and Carmen rollers.

She wound down the window and lit a cigarette and looked back to check the caravan was still attached. Liddy had cried a bit because she'd wanted to be pulled along inside the caravan instead of the car, but Uncle Colin had explained that would be dangerous.

'I don't care!' she'd said, folding her arms in that way of hers.

'What if you wanted to go to the toilet?' said Ian, and I thought that was really funny, that he'd think of that.

'Portapotty, Portapotty,' sang Liddy to herself as we hit the road and Ian pressed his thigh against mine till I felt the blood rise again in my cheeks.

We drove over the bumpy, knotty ground of the site, up on to the dirt track, past the concrete shower building. And, as the car turned, I glanced back towards the pub and the jalopy tracks which were fast turning to mud in the rain.

'Home James, and don't spare the horses!' said Uncle Colin and he slipped a tape in as we drove away from the site. It was 'Lovely Boating Weather'. We all groaned.

And Mum looked at Uncle Colin and he turned and winked at her and put his great, dad-like hand on her knee. And I thought maybe if you believed in God – or, OK, not God exactly, but Something – if you could do that, then that was all you needed to keep you steady in life.

I wondered if Ian would be a bit of a character like his dad when he grew up. I hoped he'd have better taste in music. I wondered whether brothers and sisters could go out together if they weren't properly related. Was it OK to do all that with someone when you lived with their father?

I wondered about a lot of different, unconnected things as we headed for the motorway and the rain started again. And I thought, isn't it funny – all this happiness and no one's ever managed to explain what it feels like exactly?

We've got You for Life

Anthony Masters

Greg knew how to fail his mocks. He'd worked it all out. But of course it was very different on the day, sitting in the hall that smelt of sweat and stale dinners, watching the others with their heads down, writing feverishly or staring down at the questions with blank incomprehension. *Answer one question from each section.* The instruction burnt into his mind and it was hard to defy the bleak authority of the command. *Answer one question from each section.*

No way. Greg was going to answer three questions from the *same* section. Then he was bound to fail.

He started to write, cold sweat on his brow and a sick feeling inside. Gradually, however, Greg began to feel a sense of gloomy, martyred triumph. He was failing for Dad and Mum. Because they had failed him. The rage rose up in Greg again, strong as a Rottweiler.

* * *

'How did you get on?' asked Bradley, always laid back, always successful.

'It's a weird system, isn't it?'

'What is?'

'Why divide the questions into sections when you can answer all three from one section if you want to.' Greg shrugged and waited for the predictable reaction.

'*What*?' Bradley stared at him in mounting, pleasurable horror. 'You must be an idiot. A complete raving idiot!'

'What are you getting so worked up about?' Greg asked innocently.

'I'll tell you what I'm getting worked up about,' said Bradley, scornfully. 'You're telling me you've answered three questions from the same section?'

'Yeah.'

'For each exam?'

'That's it.'

'Then you've failed the lot. You've absolutely, completely dropped yourself in it.'

'What do you mean? What have I done wrong?'

'You're meant to answer one question from each section. Not three from the same. Now you've really blown it.'

Greg shrugged and began to walk slowly and casually away, whistling tunelessly.

Bradley watched him in amazement. Why didn't Greg care?

On the way home, he wondered if he should wait until his tutor let him know the worst, or warn his parents now.

Then Greg made up his mind to tell them over supper. What he wanted was a row, the biggest row they had ever had in their lives.

The time had come for a showdown. Underneath, all he wanted to do was to cry, but that was the last thing he was going to do.

As he got nearer his house, Greg rehearsed his lines.

You shouldn't have adopted me. You only want Tom. He's the one you love. You don't love me. You never loved me. I'm second-best, that's all, just an afterthought.

The rage returned, and for the hundredth time Greg's mind worried like a dog with a bone at the cause of his misery. The Rottweiler howled.

Tom's parents had decided to adopt a baby because his mother had had such a hard time giving birth to Tom that she and Dad had decided they shouldn't have any more children. They had adopted Greg when he was only six weeks old and had always said that his arrival was just the same as when Tom came back from the hospital. He had never questioned that. Until now.

Greg and Tom had always got on all right. But that wasn't the point. Mum and Dad had been so worried about Tom's finals that it was as if they had forgotten Greg's existence. Then Tom had got a First. Now they were all celebrating and Greg felt even more left out and unwanted than ever.

Last Tuesday Tom had had his twenty-first birthday and with the birthday came the bike. The mountain bike had seemed like the final blow. Why were Mum and Dad lavishing so much time and money on Tom? Would they do the same for him? Had they *ever* done the same for him? No chance.

Greg had made no contact with his natural parents. Since the bike, however, he'd been thinking about them every day. Should he trace them? But after all, they had given him away in the first place and, anyway, it was Mum and Dad's love that he really wanted.

So Greg had decided to test them out by failing his mocks.

'I flunked.' Greg's voice was hollow as they sat round the tea table, eating one of Mum's curries. He spooned in more chutney and repeated, 'I flunked.'

The response, however, was disappointing to say the least. Dad was reading the evening paper and didn't even bother to look up. Mum was cutting more bread. Tom was away but was coming home later that night. I bet they're looking forward to that, Greg thought miserably. They don't give a damn what I do. It's Tom all the way.

Then Mum said very slowly, 'You what?'

'I flunked the mocks.'

Dad lowered his paper. Had he been listening all the time? Preparing himself?

'How do you know?' Mum demanded, the knife poised in midair.

'You have to answer one question from each section.'

They both nodded.

'Trouble is, I answered three questions from the same section. Each time. Each paper. Each exam.'

The appalled and shocked silence seemed to stretch right outside and it was as if everything had gone on hold. Greg waited for the explosion.

Instead, Dad said, 'I'm so sorry.' He put the paper down on the table. 'I'm so very sorry.'

Mum was already flinging her arms round Greg, trailing her cuff in the curry. She was always doing things like that and he felt a rush of affection for her that he tried to suppress.

'Darling – what bad luck. They ought to have made it clearer. It's not fair.'

No it's not, thought Greg, for entirely different reasons.

'Lucky it's only the mocks,' said Dad, calmly. 'You'll be OK for the real thing.'

Greg's temper rose. He had hoped for a monumental row so that he could accuse them of only caring for Tom.

But all he was getting was a game of Happy Families.

He pushed his chair back with a loud scraping sound. 'I'm not hungry.'

'Of course you're not,' said Mum.

'I'm going to my room.'

'Watch a movie,' advised Dad. 'Didn't Tom have a *Godzilla* video?'

'I don't want to watch *Godzilla*.'

'Of course you don't,' said Mum. 'You've had a terrible shock. Have a rest and I'll come up and see if you're hungry later.'

'It happens to us all,' said Dad. 'Do you want a beer?'

'No, I don't!'

Greg thundered out, slamming the door behind him, running away from their sympathy and understanding which *had* to be phoney. Didn't it?

He lay on his bed, furious. He had gone to such trouble to cause a row and all they could do was to patronise him.

Then another idea for a showdown crept into his mind. At first he rejected it completely. But the wickedness of the plan began to attract him. They wouldn't be sympathetic after what he was about to do. This time they would be absolutely furious – and so would Tom. At last he'd get his row and Greg could speak his mind.

Creeping downstairs again, he listened at the sitting room door but could only hear the chattering buzz of the

TV set. Then he heard his mother say, 'Greg really needs support, you know, Tim.'

'And we're going to be behind him all the way.' Dad sounded confident.

Stop patronising me, thought Greg viciously, as he tip-toed through the kitchen to the garage where Tom's mountain bike was leaning against the wall, gleaming in all its metallic glory.

He opened the side door as quietly as he could, grabbed the bike and rode it away.

As he pedalled through the evening streets, Greg suddenly felt the angry tears pricking at the back of his eyes. Blinking them away he pedalled even faster.

The next part of the plan began to form. He'd hide up somewhere and stay out all night. That should make them suffer! Then he'd ride back tomorrow, a lone, half-starved figure, ready to do battle.

At the top of the high street, a lane led to a patch of ragged woodland, beyond which was a steep-sided valley with an empty farmhouse at the bottom. When they were much younger, Greg and Tom had often played there, and it seemed an appropriate shelter for the night.

Greg's anger and self-pity grew until he felt cut off from the outside world, barely noticing how fast the bike was going. All he could think about was Mum and Dad and Tom sitting round the TV, probably not even realising he'd gone. Eventually one of them might start to look for him, only to find his bedroom empty and the bike missing. Would they call the police? Go looking themselves? Would they say to each other, Good riddance?

Greg was cycling through the dark scrubby woodland that was littered with old mattresses, abandoned cars and rusty machinery. Normally he would have been wary of riding here alone at night. Recently there had been a couple of rapes, and even an attempted murder.

But Greg's fury was too great for him to feel afraid: it was like a protective blanket, cutting off cold reality.

Soon he was racing downhill, leaning back in the saddle, the bike rattling beneath him, occasionally skidding on the rough ground. There was no path, only the steeply shelving sides of the valley.

Greg switched on the headlamp, and when he saw how steep the descent had become, a sudden and unexpected wave of panic filled him. What was he doing out here? What was he really trying to prove?

Then his front wheel hit an old fridge and Greg pitched over the handlebars, rolling down the hillside. He saw the tree too late to take avoiding action.

Tom's precious mountain bike followed, twisting and turning until it, too, came to a halt with a horrible grinding crunch.

Greg tried to get up but fell back with a howl of pain.

He knew he had twisted his ankle badly, but couldn't see well enough to assess any other damage. In fact, he could hardly see anything at all. Evening had become night and the landscape was dense with the all-embracing darkness. Greg only knew that he was lying against a tree on a hillside, that his ankle hurt and Tom's mountain bike lay somewhere nearby, no doubt a heap of tangled wreckage.

The silence was like clammy cotton wool around him, broken every now and then by something creaking in the light breeze – the sudden squawk of a night bird, and the scampering of a small animal reminded Greg that although the woods were scattered with discarded human debris, wild creatures still managed to lead their lives.

The pain in his ankle was getting worse. What was he going to do? How long could he survive out here before someone came to find him? But why *should* they come?

Then Greg saw a beam wavering amongst the trees and he froze. Maybe if he lay very still, he might pass unnoticed. But then he remembered the mountain bike. That would soon give him away. But he deserved it, didn't he?

The beam was now wobbling about so much that Greg was even more alarmed. Was some drunken old dosser getting nearer by the minute? Greg shivered and felt sick.

The beam wobbled even closer.

The beam caught Greg, almost blinding him, and the

stranger on the bike came to a squealing halt.

There was a long silence during which Greg lay as still as he could.

'Making a night of it then?' asked Tom.

Tom was riding Dad's old boneshaker. 'What do you think you're doing out here?'

'I've hurt my ankle.' Greg knew how angry Tom was going to be.

'Mum and Dad are out of their minds with worry. What happened?'

'I ran away.'

'Ran?'

'I mean – I cycled.'

'You cycled here on my bike?' There was a new tension in Tom's voice.

'Yes.' Greg could barely speak.

'Where is it?'

'Over there.'

Tom dismounted, detached the lamp and swung it about. Then he gave a gasp of angry dismay.

'Is it badly damaged?' Greg asked miserably.

'The chassis's bent. You're an idiot. What are you?'

'An idiot,' Greg whispered. 'I'm sorry.'

'Why did you steal my new bike?' Tom moved nearer, his fury increasing, and Greg wondered whether he was going to hit him.

He tried to evade the question. 'How did you know I'd come here?'

'I had this hunch. Don't you remember? We used to play in this wood when we were kids.'

Greg nodded. There seemed nothing more to say.

'Did you want to be found?' Tom asked in a monotone. He was suddenly calmer, clearly making an effort to hold his temper back. He came over and knelt down beside him. 'Why did you steal my bike?' he repeated.

'I wanted a row.'

'A row?' Tom was taken aback. 'Who with? Me?'

'All of you.'

'What did you want a row for?'

'So I could say things.'

'What things?'

'Like about being adopted.'

'What about being adopted?' Tom asked, without the slightest trace of anger now.

'I didn't think I was wanted.'

'I always thought you were spoilt to death and now you've not only nicked my bike but wrecked it too. What more do you want?'

'I'll buy you another one,' Greg said wildly.

'How?' Tom was scoffing.

'I'll get a job. A newspaper round. I'll work weekends – ' The ineffective words petered out.

There was a silence. Then Tom scrambled to his feet.

'Where're you going?' asked Greg fearfully.

'To get help and put Mum and Dad out of their misery.'

'Don't be long.'

Tom stood, looking down at him with a wry smile. 'You don't have to worry. We've got you for life, haven't we?' Tom rattled away, standing up on the pedals, leaving Greg in the dark.

But he wasn't afraid. Not now.

We've got you for life.

Tom's words beat in his head. Greg knew that was all the reassurance he was ever going to need. Nothing else mattered. Not now.

On the Bench

Stephen Potts

Dear Dad,

Mam's helping me write this but the words are all mine. Thanks for the football you sent for my birthday. I practise a lot against next door's wall. I'm not very good yet, but I'm getting better. I'm sorry you couldn't get off work, but it's OK. I hope the army let you off at Christmas. Which isn't long now. Please be careful with your tank and come home soon.

Love, Gary

Dear Dad,

Mam's helping me again but not so much this time. Thank

you very much for the new boots. They are great, but I don't wear them to practise against the wall because they need grass, like at the rec. It was good playing there with you and Uncle John. I hope I will be as good as him one day.

Arsenal on Boxing Day was brilliant. I really like that Bergkamp. Is that how you spell it? I jumped and shouted when he got the goal. I wish we could go to every match.

I'm sorry you had to go back to the army early, but Mam says you'll be leaving soon, and it will be better then. I hope so. Maybe when you live with us again you and Mam will not shout so much.

School starts again soon, and I'm glad. The lessons are sometimes fun but the best part is the football in the playground. On Tuesday I can take my new boots because we play in teams in the park.

Love, Gary

Dear Dad,

I saw your car so I left you a note, the traffic warden better not take it away. I haven't seen you for ages. You have to work even harder now you've left the army. I didn't know you worked near here as well. Maybe if you get a chance you could come and watch us play. Our team is quite good now and we won on Saturday. I've got to run after the others. Maybe I'll see you tonight. Can we go to Arsenal again soon?

Love, Gary

Hello? Hello, Dad? I know you're not there because you're driving around with your work, but Mam said you have a machine to take messages. It's morning break and I'm at the phone in the sweet shop. The money's going quickly so I might not have any left for crisps, but I wanted to say thank you ever so much for taking me to Highbury again. I hope Bergkamp's going to play again soon. It was good that Uncle John was there. He makes a lot of noise and he's very funny. Will you –
beep beep beep beep beep

Dear Dad,

This is the team sheet for Saturday. Here's my name. I'm supposed to be a wingback, but I don't really know what that is. It's not like the Arsenal programme but I wanted you to have it. I wanted to show you myself, but I had to go to bed because I'm tired after practice, so I'm leaving it with Mam for when you come in. See you Saturday.

Love, Gary

To: s-graham@insAB.com.uk
From: gary@stmark.com.uk

Hello Dad!

This is my first e-mail. We're doing computers now. I didn't
tell you yet. Mam got your e-mail thing but I asked her not
to say until I could use the machine. I checked with the
teacher and she said it's OK. She helped me a lot too. I hope
your boss doesn't mind. There's only one machine for all
the kids, but if you send e-mail back the teacher will show
it to me. See you tonight.

Gary

Dear Dad,

HAPPY FATHER'S DAY!

I spent ages picking this tie. Mam wanted to choose one
for me but I wouldn't let her. Your suit is dead smart, and
I like it better than the Army clothes, but there's not
enough colours in it. When you put it on, will you show

me how you tie it? You do it so quickly and I can never work it out.

I'm glad you'll be home all weekend. If the weather's good, maybe we could all go to the rec again with Uncle John. I know Mam would like to go to the park and sit by the pond, but they don't let you play football there, and last time we went the ducks bit me, remember. Anyway, whatever we do will be good.

Love, Gary

Dear Dad,

Here is my school report. Miss Johnson said I had to show it to you and Mam so you could talk about it at the meeting next week. It's not bad, I think, except for what Mr Rigby said. I don't know what mischief means, and whatever he tells you I did, I didn't. He doesn't like any of us and we don't like him. Maybe that's why he gives us all bad reports.

I don't know what's wrong with Mam. She's gone all quiet and doesn't laugh. I think its because you didn't come with her and me to the park after we played football. I was scared but the ducks were OK. Mam laughed at me when the ducks came up for bread, but she stopped laughing when I said I kept seeing your car near our

practice place. Please will you talk to her and find out
what's wrong?

Love, Gary

Dear Dad,

I'm taking this to your work because you don't come home
now. I was going to post it but I don't know where you live
and I didn't want to ask Mam. I'm going to borrow Jimmy's
bike at break and bring it there myself. I hope I will see
you, but I think you'll be out in your car.

I don't know what Mr Rigby told you but you're so
angry with me, and Mam doesn't talk since the teachers'
night, so it must have been bad. Then you and Mam
shouted so much I got scared. The glass in the door cracked
when you shut it so hard. I could hear it upstairs, and I
could hear Mam crying, but she wouldn't tell me why. I
asked her what Mr Rigby told you, but she said she didn't
know, you only came for the end part of the meeting and
Mr Rigby had gone. I don't know what I've done wrong, so
I can't make it right. If you can't come home and tell me
please come to practice tomorrow. I can stay after for a
while. But please don't be angry.

Love, Gary

Dear Dad,

Your secretary lady was very nice to me when I brought the letter to your work, and she showed me how to write the envelope to where you live now, but I don't know why she came with you to watch us play. Does she like football? I said to Mam you were there. She went sad again, and asked if you were on your own. I said no and made her cry. I'm glad you are not angry with me now, but I don't think you should be angry with Mam.

We're playing again on Saturday. I would like it if you could come but please don't bring that lady.

Love, Gary

Dear Dad,

Thanks for putting the Arsenal ticket through the door. I didn't get it till after the match because Uncle John and Aunty Pat took Mam and me to the seaside for the whole weekend. It was great. I sent you a postcard but you'll get this first. Uncle John and me went in a boat and we fished off the pier and we played football on the beach. Mam and Aunty Pat sat in deckchairs and talked and talked. When we got back from the boat Mam's eyes were red but she was laughing like she hasn't done for a long time. She bought us all fish and chips after.

We're playing in the semi-final soon, and I hope you will come. Uncle John showed me how to bend the ball, like at free kicks. Maybe I will get a chance to show you.

Love, Gary

Dear Dad,

It's not as sunny as on the picture but it's good fun all the same. We're sitting at the bottom of the cliff, where I put the cross, like in spot-the-ball. Uncle John and me are going in a boat soon, round to the rocks at the edge of the picture. We've already been fishing on the pier but I didn't catch anything. Maybe I will, on the boat.

Mam's talking with Aunty Pat. She doesn't know I'm sending this. Will you take her to the pictures on her birthday, like you did last year?

Love, Gary

Dear Dad,

I'm glad you came to watch us and sorry that when I did the free kick it wouldn't bend. It does when I practise, honest. The final is in two weeks. We practise every day now, and the whole school's really excited. All the girls want to talk to us. It's funny, they never talked to me before.

Thank you for not bringing that secretary lady. I didn't want to meet her after, like you said, because I had to get back for tea. Uncle John and Aunty Pat were coming round and Mam said not to be late. Uncle John said he'd take me to Arsenal Saturday. Mam surprised us all when she said she wanted to come too. She said that's all she wants for her birthday this year, but I'm going to get her another book about making bracelets and things. She's started doing that again and she sold some at the car boot sale on Sunday. She bought me a Bergkamp shirt with the money.

I didn't like it when you said that lady was my new mam. I hope you don't call her that when I'm not there. I won't tell Mam you said it, and maybe it's best if you don't come to Arsenal with us.

Love Gary

Dad? Are you there? Hello? Well, I'll just talk to your machine. The Arsenal game was good. Mam loved it. She shouts even more than me. Was it OK for you watching it on TV? When you came to watch us practise yesterday the teachers were really rushing us back to school, so I didn't

get time to talk to you enough. I've thought about what
you said, about bringing that lady to watch us in the final.
Well I don't want her to come. Mam and Aunty Pat and
Uncle John will all be there. If you're going to bring that
lady with you I don't want you to come. I want —
beep beep beep beeep beeeeeeeeeeeeeeeeeep

Coming Home

Melvin Burgess

I'd come home early from school. It was a hot day. I let myself in and went to the kitchen to get some juice out of the fridge. As I stood there swigging orange out of the carton I looked out of the kitchen window and there, tucked down behind the shed, was my mum having a snog with some bloke. They were dappled with shadow from the trees. Her blouse was unbuttoned, hanging open. They were kissing each other very hard, and he kept crushing her up into his chest and sliding his hands under her blouse at the back and on her shoulders.

I ducked out of sight. I felt a bit like James Bond, hiding there with my back to the wall, the carton of juice in my hand like a gun. Then I peeped round again to have another look. I wanted to watch, I wanted to see if he was going to take her clothes off.

They were smiling now. She put her hands round his face and kissed him in a way I never saw her kiss my dad. It was like a film. It was so unreal, it made me think of fairies at the bottom of the garden. I felt that if I took a picture of it, it wouldn't come out. He pushed her up against the shed wall and slid his hands down to her bum. I could see her hands stroking the back of his neck.

I walked back to the front door, opened it, slammed it hard, and then wandered about shouting, 'I'm home, Mum, I'm home! Mum, I'm home!' at the top of my voice. I went back into the kitchen and pretended to get the juice out of the fridge again and didn't look out of that window.

'Mum, I'm home!' I bellowed. I went into the sitting room and turned on the TV. There was nothing on. It was only half past two. We'd been let out of school early. Mum should have been at work. There was a schools program about geology and I watched that.

They came into the house a couple of minutes later. I could hear their voices.

'. . . yes, nice to see you.'

'And you. We'll get that trip organised, then.'

'OK.'

'Right . . .'

'Cup of tea?'

'No, better go . . .'

They walked down the hall and stopped outside the door. Mum's head popped in.

'You're home early, Laurence,' she said.

'So are you.'

'They let us off early.'

'Same here.'

Outside the door a voice called, 'Hi, Laurence.'

'Oh, hi, Nigel.' Nigel Turner. Mr Turner. Someone from her school. There was a pause and then he said, 'I better be off, Sandra.' She walked him to the door. I ran to the window to see him. I caught him standing right next to his car, and he looked over his shoulder full into my face but I didn't run away or even flinch. We stared at each other for a second, then he opened the car door and got in, and I went back to the TV.

Mum came back and said, 'Hello, darling, good day?'

'Sure.'

She said, 'How did you know I was home, Laurence?'

'Dunno,' I said.

I could feel her staring at me.

'Must've seen your bag or something.'

'You're home early,' she said again.

For the first time I looked up at her. She tried to smile. I smiled back but my face must have looked like a cartoon. I looked back at the telly and waited while she left the room.

I thought, she knows I know, and I know she knows I know. I expected her to have a little talk with me, which is what usually happens in our house if there're any problems, but she never said a thing about it. She was scared . . . You see? Chicken.

My sister Gill came home later and we sat and watched TV and ate crisps together, but I never said anything to her about it. She's sixteen, two years older than me and she's always giving me advice about girls.

Once I said to her, 'What do you know about girls?'

And she said, 'I *am* a girl.'

'Not a proper one,' I said.

She got up in a huff. 'Can't you take anything seriously?' she snapped.

'Only if it's worth it,' I said, and she rolled her eyes and stamped out. But I was being serious, she *doesn't* know anything about girls, not the kind of girls I want to go out with. The kind of girls I want to go out with would *like* me talking like that.

I once caught my mum and dad having sex, you know. I went into the room without knocking and she was sitting on top of him. I hadn't thought at the time but looking back I could hear her making pleased sounding noises before I went in. I didn't really know what it was at the time, but Gill told me. She said it must have been. It didn't look anything like what she was doing with this other bloke, though. That was like a film, or something you just thought, but it never really happened.

The day after I saw her and Nigel Turner I remember

standing by my bedroom window, which is above the kitchen, looking down into the garden where they'd been and saying to myself, 'She has a lover,' but I still couldn't make it as though it had really happened. I said, 'Sandra,' to myself. We always called her Mum. Even though that woman down there with her blouse open had been my mum, it wasn't the same person who cooked and worked and shopped and woke up every morning smelling of dad.

When I was younger, a few years ago, I used to try and see my mum with nothing on. I used to peep through the keyhole of the bedroom . . . well, I'd never seen a real woman in the nude. I hadn't done it for years but now I wanted to see her like that again. I was handing the dishes to her after dinner a few days later. I was fed up thinking about it whenever I saw her. She still hadn't said anything to me. She was bending over putting the plates in the dishwasher and I was looking at her back. I was thinking . . . what was it that made Nigel Turner so turned on? She had on this slightly transparent blouse; you could see her bra strap under it, and where the flesh squeezed out on either side. I reached down, I took the strap in my fingers and I snapped it.

She looked up at me as if I'd hit her. 'What did you do that for, Laurence?' she snapped.

I shrugged. 'I dunno.' Well, I didn't know . . . I just did it.

She scowled; she was really furious. She stood up and

yelled in my face, 'You're not to do that to me again. Do you understand?'

'Yeah, sure, so what?'

Then she stamped off out of the room. I was really angry. It was just a joke. It didn't mean anything, it was a joke. Maybe I did it harder than I meant to. I thought she should be grateful to me really. I could have said if I'd wanted. I thought, what would happen if I told my dad?

It was at dinner. Dad always says, 'The family that eats together, stays together.' He did nearly all the cooking ever since he went part-time at the school where he teaches. He used to be Head of English but it was too much work for him. Now he thinks how lucky we all are because we can have home-cooked food three or four times during the week and not just at weekends. Sometimes he even bakes bread. The bread's nice, and sometimes he does nice meals but I prefer meals out of a packet.

Someone said my name.

'What?'

'Pass the sauce, cloth-ears,' said Gill.

'Sorry.'

I had this plan about making loads of money by blackmailing my mum. I could threaten to tell my dad unless she gave me loads of money. I could make her write her will out in my favour. I could make her give me tenners whenever I wanted. Then Gill would always be saying,

'Where did you get all that?' and I'd just go, 'Ah ha! Nothing for noses,' like she does to me whenever I ask her anything.

'Laurence!'

'What?'

'Not what, pardon.'

'What?'

'Christ. Do you want more fish pie?'

'No, thanks.'

'You're in a dream.'

I *was* in a dream. I could make a fortune. Out of Nigel Turner, too. He was married. I think he and his wife had even come to dinner sometime. I could blackmail both of them. I'd be the richest kid in the school. I could have anything I liked. It was great.

Mum and Dad started bickering. Dad wanted Mum to go part-time, like him. He was saying it was too much stress working full-time at a school these days. He was saying how bad tempered and distant she was. He was always going on about all these other teachers who were having nervous breakdowns and falling to bits, and that she should get out and go part-time before it happened to her and he was left having to pay all the bills on half a wage and run the house all on his own.

'We could have days out. We could walk or visit places. Look . . . I can do anything I want on Mondays, Tuesdays and Friday afternoons. You could do it with me,' he said.

'But I *like* working full time,' she said.

'Well, I think it's selfish of you,' said my dad. 'Life's to enjoy, not to work yourself into the ground.'

'I'm not working myself into the ground.'

'Then why are you so distant? If you're married with a family, you ought to be prepared to spend a bit of time with them.'

Gill said he only went on like that because he couldn't bear Mum being better at work than he was. She said, 'He couldn't take it. Men are weaker than women, really.' Well, I dunno. Dad used to be good at everything. He never had to work hard, it always came out right for him.

The other really great thing about Mum having an affair was that I had it in my hands like a time bomb or a grenade or something. I could pull the pin and let it go. I could blow up the family! Or I could quietly sit on it, show it to my mum . . . and make my fortune. It was like a weapon. I'd never really thought before about knowledge as being dangerous like that. When you know certain kinds of things, it's like power. It lets you do things you could never have done before. I started thinking about how to ask Mum to put my pocket money up. It was a start.

'What's wrong with you?' yelled my dad. I think I heard him but I assumed he was talking to my mum. There was a pause. He got really cross and he bawled, 'I said, what's the matter with you, Laurence?' When he said my name I almost jumped out of my chair.

'What?'

'What? What all the time! Get a grip, will you? What's the matter?'

I looked at my mum. She blushed. She blushed! It was suddenly like it was all out in the open. *I* blushed. My dad was staring at me, scowling away. Then he noticed my mum as red as a tomato and all his anger went and he looked shocked.

Then I started acting stupid. I don't know what was going through my head. I was fed up with keeping it a secret, I wanted to tell someone and it suddenly occurred to me that it didn't matter if I did. I mean, so what? People have affairs all the time. It was a joke!

I leaned across to my mum and I said, 'Give us a kiss, Sandra.' And I blew her a kiss and winked. It was the wink that did it. It was a long, slow lecherous wink and it served her right.

I didn't mean to. Maybe I was getting messed up with the game and real life, because although I liked thinking about making all that money, it was like the other ways I've had of getting rich – they never work in the end. Listen, she should have had one of her little talks with me. She should have said something. She just left it up to me, and I'm a child still, right? And . . . she shouldn't have hit me.

Suddenly my mum swung forward and slapped me round my face as hard as she could. It went . . . crack! It really hurt. I put my hand to my cheek and it felt red-hot and smooth.

I didn't actually tell, even then. I just said, 'You shouldn't have done that,' like it was a threat.

Dad jumped up. He was really angry. 'Or what?' he yelled. 'Or what?'

I ignored him and I said to my mum, 'I didn't tell. So what did you hit me for?' and I nodded at Dad, just so it was clear who I hadn't told.

Everything was very quiet. I could see my dad licking his lips. Then Mum said, 'You and Gill better go upstairs. Your dad and me need to talk.'

Gill said, 'But we haven't finished.'

'Just go upstairs for half an hour. Both of you. Go on.'

Gill tutted and groaned, but we got up to go. Mum looked up at me and said, 'Happy?'

We got upstairs, and I made to go into my room, but Gill grabbed hold of me and said, 'What's going on? What's *wrong* with you?' I didn't want to but she made me tell her everything. Afterwards, she thought I was the most stupid person in the whole world. She started to shout at me, which was a bit much after I'd told her everything. It made me incredibly angry, it was so unfair. I screamed and shouted, I was so angry, and I threw her out of my room. Afterwards, I could hear her crying next door.

Of course, I got the little talk *then*. Then she was right up the stairs, my mum, telling me how it wasn't my fault, but it was all too late then, wasn't it? Anyway, she was only saying that, she never believed it. Gill thought it was my fault all right, she never stopped going on about it. Mum and Dad were always saying how it wasn't my fault at all, but even they say I should have spoken to Mum about it first. But I never let it out, did I? I didn't actually say anything about it.

They were down there for ages. We never did get our pudding. After a while, they started shouting. It went on for ages, and then the next night and the next . . . it just kept on.

The thing that gets me is the way it all just fell to pieces. I don't think they even tried. My dad had it coming, actually. He's always been the smart one, the good looking one, the clever one. He's one of those people, everything they do is perfect . . . it makes you sick. And then when things do go wrong he can't take it! And he's had affairs . . . he admitted it. Can you believe that? Gill heard them talking about it. You know what he said to Gill when she accused him of being a hypocrite? He said, 'Yes, but that was just mucking about. Your mother is *in love*.'

The day she left he was working in the garden. All along the bottom of the garden there's a long row of poplar trees. He's been on about them for years. He says poplar trees have robbing roots, which is why nothing grows well in our garden – they steal all the goodness out of the soil. You can find the roots just under the surface almost anywhere in our garden. So on this day, the day she left, he started to dig a trench right across the end of the garden to cut through all the roots growing our way.

Mum said she really wanted to stay but they had to split up, so she gave him the choice and he chose to stay on at the family home. She said it made more sense because he was the one who was going to be spending more time at home, so he was better able to look after us. Gill said he should have stayed away while Mum was moving her stuff out, but instead of doing that he went into the back garden straight after breakfast. He spent the whole day there, digging this trench. Mum was popping in and out with boxes.

You know what . . . she made me and Gill help. Well, she tried, anyway. Gill just said no. She went into town. I did a couple of boxes, and then I went into my room and sat by the window watching Dad dig his trench. He just worked and worked. Gradually he went deeper into the ground.

About lunch-time I opened the window and shouted out at the top of my voice so everyone could hear, 'Why don't you do something? Why don't you *stop* her?' I saw him lift his head up and stare at me, but then he just went back on with his spade. By evening you could just see the top of his head poking out of the top, bobbing up and down as he dug.

Mum went about tea-time. She said she'd see us tomorrow at her new place for tea.

'It's just up the road, we can see each other whenever we want,' she said. Then she drove off to Nigel. Later, Gill came home and we went out to the garden to see Dad. He stood at the bottom of this trench. It was amazing it was so deep. I hung around by the shed while she put her hand out to him.

'Coming in, Dad?' she said.

'Has she gone?'

'She's gone.'

He ignored her hand and pulled himself up a ladder he had down at one end of the trench. He was all streaked with mud. He looked hopeless. Pathetic. I'd have liked to push him back in the bloody trench and fill the earth in on top of him, he was so useless.